SIX-GUN GAMBLE

A gun roared its death notice. Dust spattered inches from Malloy's boot. The big-boned gambler hit the dirt and held his body rigid. Twenty yards ahead was the safety of his cabin. But behind him was the bushwhacking killer who had dogged his trail relentlessly. Malloy squirmed a foot closer to the cabin on his belly. 'That's right, Malloy—crawl!' It was Tony Balter, all right. 'Dig a hole and climb into it! I'll pick you off when I'm ready!' Like an echo, another slug slammed the ground near Malloy's head. 'Here it comes, Malloy!' his enemy shouted. Tensely, the gambler waited for death . . .

D(wight) B(ennett) Newton is the author of a number of notable Western novels. Born in Kansas City, Missouri, Newton went on to complete work for a Master's degree in history at the University of Missouri. From the time he first discovered Max Brand in Street and Smith's *Western Story Magazine*, he knew he wanted to be an author of Western fiction. He began contributing Western stories and novelettes to the Red Circle group of Western pulp magazines published by Newsstand in the late 1930s. During the Second World War, Newton served in the US Army Engineers and fell in love with the central Oregon region when stationed there. He would later become a permanent resident of that state and Oregon frequently serves as the locale for many of his finest novels. As a client of the August Lenniger Literary Agency, Newton found that every time he switched publishers he was given a different byline by his agent. This complicated his visibility. Yet in notable novels from *Range Boss* (1949), the first original novel ever published in a modern paperback edition, through his impressive list of titles for the Double D series from Doubleday, *The Oregon Rifles, Crooked River Canyon,* and *Disaster Creek* among them, he produced a very special kind of Western story. What makes it so special is the combination of characters who seem real and about whom a reader comes to care a great deal and Newton's fundamental humanity, his realization early on (perhaps because of his study of history) that little that happened in the West was ever simple but rather made desperately complicated through the conjunction of numerous opposed forces working at cross purposes. Yet, through all of the turmoil on the frontier, a basic human decency did emerge. It was this which made the American frontier experience so profoundly unique and which produced many of the remarkable human beings to be found in the world of Newton's Western fiction.

SIX-GUN GAMBLE

D. B. Newton

GUNSMOKE

This hardback edition 2006
by BBC Audiobooks Ltd
by arrangement with
Golden West Literary Agency

ISBN 10: 1 4056 8084 9
ISBN 13: 978 1 405 68084 4

British Library Cataloguing in Publication Data available.

Printed and bound in Great Britain by
Antony Rowe Ltd., Chippenham, Wiltshire

1

Like the town itself, Mark Malloy had slept through the whole of this hot summer's afternoon. Waking at sunset, he stepped forth now upon spur-scored sidewalk plankings—dressed and shaven, his cheeks tingling to the razor's clean sting. An evening breeze had begun to stir, bringing with it the parched scent of sage and distant desert. Malloy bit the tip off a long cheroot from his waistcoat pocket, and paused to take a leisurely survey of Saunderstown.

He did not much resemble the occasional cowhand who moved by him with swish of chaps and clump of heavy cowhides. The shirt he wore was of fine white linen, soft-collared, complete with black string tie. Malloy's tweed suitcoat and carefully creased trousers were tailor fitted; the low-heeled boots, benchmade and rubbed up to a dazzle. Looking at his clothing, and at the not-unhandsome face with its carefully trimmed mustache, you would hardly have guessed that a bird of ill fortune sat heavily upon this man's shoulder, digging in its long, sharp claws.

Actually, Malloy had reached the sour suspicion that his present surroundings were, to all intents and purposes, hexed for him. It was certainly a fact that, in three days here, a good-sized roll had dwindled dangerously, and with no sign as yet of any break in his disastrous run of luck. . . .

A man who carried a black medical bag came plodding up from the livery barn; a tired-looking, gray-haired figure, probably just returned from answering a call somewhere on the fringes of a widespread country practice. Malloy had once or twice exchanged the time of day with Doc Reading, whose office adjoined his own room at the hotel. He nodded

5

a greeting and got a tired reply. The doctor halted beside him.

Reading said, "So your day's beginning; while mine's just ended—I hope. Odd hours you keep, friend."

"Gamblers, footpads, and night watchmen," Malloy agreed. Absently he put a hand to his eyes and pressed the lids, shaking his head and blinking a time or two.

The doctor noted the gesture with quick professional interest. "They hurt?"

"Burn a little." Malloy shrugged. "It's nothing important; they get that way."

"I dunno. A person wants to look out for his eyes. You abuse 'em you know—staring at the pasteboards by lamplight, and doing what sleeping you can manage by day. Better be careful, or these all-night sessions will finish you."

"Hazards of the profession, Doc."

The other shook his head. "A blind man ain't much of a poker player. Why don't you drop in to the office tomorrow and let me have a look?"

Malloy favored him with an amused, sidelong glance. "Drumming up business?"

"For that, you can go to blazes!"

Malloy grinned. "I was only funning," he said. "I'll remember, Doc. If they keep bothering, I might be in, one of these times. . . ."

An hour or so after this, having dined sparingly at a greasy lunchroom counter, he stepped from settling dusk into the largest of Saunderstown's three saloons and was immediately hailed by one of a trio waiting at the bar.

"Here's our man!" said the cattle buyer, big Bob Osgood —a bluff, heavy-handed characer, who had been the chief instrument of Malloy's misfortunes since he hit this town. "We're ready if you are, Malloy—and if you got anything left in your poke that you want taken away from you!"

"There's a little, I guess," said Malloy, determined not to show his irritation, or to wince as the other clapped his shoulder with a meaty palm.

"Boys, you're lookin' at a rare critter." Osgood told his

companions. "An honest tinhorn, no less—a man who must know every trick of the trade, and yet plays a hard, clean game even with the string against him! Malloy, here's what I've rounded up for us tonight." And he introduced the other pair.

One was a rancher from down below Cross Timbers, a dour-faced man named Chris Henning who acknowledged the meeting with suspicion—obviously in no hurry to believe good of any professional gambler. The third man, whose name Malloy didn't even catch, was a drygoods drummer off the evening stage; he already had done considerable business in wet goods at the bar and was talking thickly and boisterously, pulling money out of his pockets.

"Le's get goin'!" this one demanded, both hands bristling with greenbacks. Malloy knew a faint stirring of interest. Normally he would have scrupled against taking on so easy a mark, but the man plainly wouldn't be happy until someone had relieved him of his money and Malloy was not in any position to refuse to accommodate him.

"We might as well start, then," he said. He wondered just how long the drummer would last. . . .

The drummer lasted, as it developed, most of two hours. But when he rose from the table, finally shorn, and went reeling out of the private room behind the bar, he had only proved that Mark Malloy's luck was even sourer than he had suspected; for Osgood and Henning had split the drummer's roll between them. Malloy supposed he could have had a share, by taking the opportunity now and again to try his hand at bottom-dealing. But such was not his brand of card playing. He was a gambler—not a blackleg.

And now his own pile of cash had dwindled well below the danger point, and within him was a nauseous unease that only the greatest discipline kept from showing upon his professionally calm exterior.

Bob Osgood, finished counting his winnings, shifted bulky weight and laid a good-humored glance on Malloy. "The game's getting smaller. And a couple of hands more ought to have *you* cleaned, huh?"

"Maybe," said Malloy, shortly. "Maybe not."

Chris Henning rose. "Drinks?" he suggested.

Malloy shook his head, but the cattle buyer was agreeable. And while the rancher from Cross Timbers went out to the bar with his order. Mark Malloy took advantage of this moment's break to put down the cards and step to the alley door, for a breath of air.

Men playing large poker do not like distractions and, despite the closeness of the atmosphere, the single window was closed and shade-pulled, the door tight shut. He swung it wide and stood a moment in the opening looking out at a starry night, while welcome coolness ran into the room and stirred the layers of blue and acrid tobacco smoke. The town was quiet tonight, with the hush of the wide, encircling prairie and the rimming hills. Down at the shipping pens, a steer bawled now and then.

Breaking out one of his pencil-thin black cheroots, Malloy bit and spat out the end, struck a match against the edge of the door jamb to light it. His eyes were smarting and he squeezed them tight, thinking vaguely, *Wonder if the doc could be right, at that.* . . .

This wasn't his main worry, however; for not far distant he could see the shaping up of a momentous decision. Around his waist, beneath his outer clothing, lay the money belt which held his reserve—exactly one thousand dollars in cash. One more losing hand—two, possibly—and he would have to make up his mind about dipping into the pockets of that hidden belt.

Down the years it had been a tenet of his superstitious gambler's religion never to touch this reserve, holding it intact against some last and desperate need. So far, the moment had never come. But tonight, he felt with increasing dread, might be the time. . . .

"You dealing, Malloy?"

Chris Henning had returned with a new bottle and the other two were waiting. Slowly, Mark Malloy closed the alley door and went back to his chair beneath the cone of light from the hanging lamp. He seated himself; carefully tended to the knife-sharp crease at the knees of his tailored trousers, and picked up the deck. The cards began to make a liquid whispering as, expressionless of face, he shuffled with practiced fingers.

He was throwing them out, five around, when the door to the bar swung suddenly open and a newcomer came bursting into the room.

The players glanced up, startled. Breathing hard, the intruder had slammed the door and set his shoulders against it, to stare about him in the murky lampglow. He was a bony figure, unshaven, his levis and red-checked shirt and leather brush jacket thickly coated with trail dust. Though he had a gun strapped to his gaunt thigh and a raw, red-knuckled hand was clamped over the butt of it, he didn't appear to be a stickup—he seemed, in fact, too wildly excited over some unnamed matter even to notice the piles of coins and bills upon the table.

Obviously neither of Malloy's companions knew him, either. It was Chris Henning who said sharply, "This is a private game, mister. Do you suppose maybe you came through the wrong door?"

The man jerked his head about, jarred by the question; he seemed aware for the first time that he was not alone. Touching tongue to dry lips, he scuttled a hasty glance across the faces of the three who sat beneath the cone of lamplight, peered past them toward the window with its drawn blind, and the closed outer door.

"Alley's that way," said Henning, "if that's what you're looking for." His tone was rimmed with impatience. "Say, what in blazes *do* you want, anyway?"

The man cleared his throat, made an indistinct sound that was no answer.

Big Osgood, however, had drunk just enough and won just enough to put him in an expansive mood. "Maybe he's lookin' for a game," he suggested. "One empty chair, mister, if you think you can stand the tariff. Stakes are pretty high, though."

Scowling, Henning protested quickly. "Now, hold on a second! We don't even know this guy—"

"Aw, what difference? I'll soon have the pair of you cleaned out and be needing somebody else to take. How about it, fellow—you want to sit in? Got some money on you?"

The stranger took the cue. "Yeah," he muttered, finding his voice at last. "Sure, I got a little—"

"Why, hell, then!" boomed Osgood; and shoving a boot under the table, he kicked back the empty chair. It struck an empty bottle and sent it spinning across the floor and into a corner.

Hesitantly, as though still looking for a rebuff, the stranger moved over and dropped a hand upon the back of the chair. Henning was scowling but withholding further comment; Mark Malloy, for his part, had already scooped in the cards and started tossing them out again—four hands, this time. Dragging a deep breath, the newcomer pulled the chair out and let himself into it. But the way he sat, it looked to Malloy's curious glance that he was tensed and ready to leap to his feet again at any moment.

Osgood made introductions. The stranger mumbled a name that sounded like Ed Renke; and as the cattle buyer poured a drink and shoved it over he snatched the glass and drained it hurriedly. Malloy, who never mixed liquor with the serious business of card playing, noted this with severe disapproval; if he wanted a drink during the course of a game, he went to the bar for it—he would not allow a glass to sit at his elbow, as a temptation, while he tried to concentrate on the fall of the pasteboards.

Big Osgood had no such compunctions. He poured himself a shot of rye and threw it off as he was reaching for his cards with the free hand, then thumbed them into a fan. "Open for fifty," he grunted.

Money plopped into the center of the table; the stranger at Osgood's left hesitating a moment before contributing from a wad of bills out of his pocket. With a silent prayer to the god of gamblers to break his streak of rotten luck,

Mark Malloy gathered his own cards and spread them out one by one.

He had a pair of nines; a king; two low cards. This was no improvement! Nevertheless, he cut into his diminishing pile to the extent of fifty dollars. "Cards, gentlemen?" he offered.

When the rest had filled their hands he discarded his two low cards, and found that he had drawn another nine. Not a strong three-of-a-kind, naturally; but still the best he had held in two hours of play. He took a slow breath, and glanced around the table.

Big Osgood threw out a couple of double-eagles from a stack in front of him. "How about this, just to get things started?"

The stranger fingered his roll of bills and then, with that impulsive gesture Malloy had noted before, made his decision and shoved money into the pot. "Call you," he said, hoarsely. "And raise you a hundred!"

He'd burned two cards; that sounded suspiciously like three-of-a-kind, and probably a higher three than Malloy's. Chris Henning without a word met the raise, though Malloy doubted that the Cross Timbers rancher held more than two pair at best. Renke was the threat. And, quickly sizing up the stranger as a cautious player who could be frozen out if the going got too quickly steep, Malloy decided on his strategy.

"How much left in that wad of bills?" he demanded. "I'll match it!"

A flush began to creep up through the other's bony face, as he stared across the table at Malloy. The gaunt fingers twitched. "Two hundred and forty," he shot back. "If that's how you play!"

"That's how I play," answered Mark Malloy, and calmly counted out the exact amount.

His face had never been more carefully expressionless. The maneuver had left him with his own pile reduced almost to nothing, but it was a bluff which he hoped might freeze Renke out.

Big Osgood, however, had ideas of his own. "Oh, hell! I hope we can do better than this!" He flung a huge fistful of coins and bills into the center of the table, and lifted an eyebrow at Renke. "Kind of rough, pal. We told you the stakes was high; I wouldn't asked you to sit in, if I'd known this was all the farther you could go along with us!"

Anger coloring his gaunt face, the stranger had raised halfway out of his chair. From the other side of him, Chris Henning added drily, "Yeah! Unless you got something more you can put up, it looks like you're finished." He jerked his head toward the door behind him. "The alley still lies yonder. Better get going—and next time, look how deep the water is before you jump in!"

Turning slowly, the stranger peered about, into cold and unfriendly eyes; even Osgood, it seemed, had lost his whiskey-born cordiality. Suddenly, Mark Malloy felt an unexpected twinge of pity.

"Why not let him draw his money back from the pot, and leave?" he suggested, gruffly. "Do we want to clean a man before he's even played out the first hand?"

"Nothing doing!" cried Henning, the flat of a palm striking the table. "He busted in here, wished himself into somebody else's game. I say he can just let his dough lay where it is!"

Malloy saw that Osgood's hard stare seconded this veto; and figuring he had done what he could he shrugged and let the matter drop.

Now Renke had pushed up from the table, a dull and beaten look on him. He looked over at the closed alley door; hesitated, his bony hand on the back of the chair tightening until the knuckles showed white beneath the stretched skin. He acted as though utterly unable to move, with his narrow chest lifting to strained breathing.

And all at once, Mark Malloy understood.

He thought, *Why, the man's scared to leave—scared of something he knows is waiting outside. Waiting, maybe, to kill him. . . .*

2

So strong was this thought that Malloy laid his cards down, looking at the man in quickened interest. But now Renke whirled about again, a feverish glint in his eyes that spoke of some new idea that might yet save him.

"Just a minute," he exclaimed. "I got something here that's worth money—a lot of money. I'll put it into the pot if you gents will match it with cash."

"Yeah?" Osgood sounded dubious. "Well, we might take a look."

With fumbling fingers Renke dug into a hip pocket and brought out a wad of folded paper that was badly crumpled and sweat-stained. He smoothed it out, dropped it onto the table in front of the other men. He said, with eager haste, "It's a patent to a proved-up piece of homestead land—title clear, no encumbrances. It's worth at least a thousand."

The others looked at the paper. Chris Henning picked it up, glanced over the description of the land, the signatures, the government seal. "Seems to be in order," he agreed. "Dunno, though, why I'd want to risk any thousand dollars of my money against an unimproved homestead quarter section."

"But it's valuable land," Renke insisted. "There's water on it—a good spring, that don't go dry. You ain't risking anything."

Osgood said, "Where is the homestead?"

"Seems to be over in the Hermit Flats country," said Henning. "Know anything about that range?"

The big man shook his head. "No, except I've heard it's dry graze."

13

"That's right," agreed Renke, eagerly. "That's entirely right. And this patent controls Indian Springs—one of the few good water sources on the edge of the Hermit Hills. There's men who'll give a good price for it; a sight more than the thousand I'm asking."

"Lemme see," said Osgood.

He took the paper from Henning, briefly, then passed it over to Mark Malloy. It was stiff with sweat, the ink smeared; but it named Edward J. Renke as holder of the proved-up land. The patent was new—dated less than a month previously.

Malloy tossed it back into the center of the table. "Suits me, I guess," he said. "Can't figure what I'd do with a homestead; still, I don't mind if he wants to play it and the rest of you are agreeable."

"But at four dollars on the acre—no more!" said Henning, flatly. "Six forty or nothing, Renke. I'll go no higher."

The other hesitated, his thin lips twitching; but then impulsively he accepted. "All right, if you'll guarantee to close the pot there. I've nothin' else left to bet."

"A deal," said Osgood, heavily, and began to count out bills from the pile in front of him. "Sit down, mister! You're called. You must be damn sure of the cards you're holding!"

With the air of one who has been granted a reprieve, Renke turned his back on that dreaded door yonder and slid again into his chair; his fingers nervously touched the cards he'd laid down, his feverish gaze moved between the faces of the other players as new bills plumped into the scatter of money at the center of the table, where the crumpled legal paper lay.

For Mark Malloy, it was a moment of decision. He had nothing like six hundred and forty dollars left in that slim stack of bills before him; to stay in the hand, he would have to do the thing he had never before permitted himself—tap the pockets of the money belt which held his last-defense stakes. This thought touched a deep, atavistic dread somewhere within his gambling man's superstitious being. It put cold fingers along his spine as he held swift inward debate.

After all, some three thousand dollars cash was on the table now, in addition to Renke's homestead patent. It would more than wipe out his losses and these three nines in his hand were the best cards he had held yet. What made him hesitate was a near conviction that Renke must also be holding three-of-a-kind, or better. . . .

He shrugged. "One moment, gentlemen."

Unbuttoning his fancy waistcoat and shirt Malloy reached in to unfasten a pocket of the money belt. He brought out from it a flat fold of bills, counted them, and with an easy gesture flipped them into the pot. "All right—suppose we look at your cards!"

Probably no one but another professional gambler could have sensed what lay beneath the surface, as he calmly redid the buttons of vest and shirt front. The others were watching Renke, now; and the man's gaunt face had split suddenly into a twisted grin of triumph.

"I got an idea it's mine," said Renke; he spread his cards in front of him. "Aces, backed by sevens. Can any of you top that?"

There was a moment's silence.

"Well, I'm damned!" growled Bob Osgood. "I thought my own two pair had it cinched—but Jacks was the highest I could go."

Chris Henning, with a grimace, had merely flung his cards into the discard. Quietly, and as casually as he could, Mark Malloy laid down his three nines.

He didn't want to show these men just what the winning or losing of this one pot had meant to him; he felt it indicated a troubling weakness lying somewhere back of his polished and unruffled exterior. With chagrin he realized that he had allowed the slim cheroot between his lips to go out, and he paused now to light it, not saying anything while he struck a match beneath the table's rim and set it to the weed. His fingers were dangerously near to trembling.

Renke had already reached forth bony hands, on the verge of raking green bills and coins toward his gaunt belly, when he happened to see Malloy's cards. That stopped him, like a sledging mule kick. His mouth sagged a little; his arms dropped back to the table, not touching the money he had thought was his. He stared at the trio of nines, and then lifted his blank stare to Malloy's face.

"Sorry, friend," murmured the gambler. He took the cheroot from his lips, inspected the burning end, and replaced it. "That's life—we all have to take our chances. Frankly, I really thought you had me bested. I'm about as surprised as you are." With a disarming smile, he began to stack up the green bills.

Bob Osgood said, heavily, "It sure as hell beats all! Who else needs a drink on that one?"

Liquor gurgled in the neck of the bottle as he poured. He shoved a filled glass toward Renke, but the man did not seem even to notice it—only sat staring fixedly at the table top before him.

Mark Malloy had his winnings collected. First of all, he carefully counted out a certain amount and folded it, tucked it into a pocket of his waistcoat; this would be replaced later in the money belt.

His face didn't show it, but he felt as one does who draws back safely from the dizzy edge of a precipice. That had been close—too close. It had been a punishment to the nerves; and now that the tension was removed he became aware of a tiredness all through him, and of the ache of his smarting, burning eyes.

Lastly, he picked up the patent to the Indian Springs claim, and as he did so felt Renke's stare lift and fasten on him. He glanced at the man across the edge of the paper.

"I'll write you out a bill of sale," Renke said.

"Hold on," said Malloy. "I'm not real sure I want this." He tossed the paper from him. "I got no use for homestead land. And winning a man's spare cash is a little different from cleaning him of the result of five years' labor. Keep it, friend."

But Renke only repeated, with dogged firmness, "I'll write you a bill of sale." Malloy, frowning, had the odd feeling that this stranger had reached a decision. It seemed almost as though, for some reason, Renke suddenly *wanted* to be rid of the deed.

"Who's got writin' materials?" the stranger demanded harshly.

Digging into a coat pocket, Chris Henning fetched out a chewed pencil stub and a dog-eared tally book from which he tore a blank sheet; he shoved these toward Renke and the man snatched them, began to write hastily.

Malloy's eyes were hurting him again; the words scrawled on the paper, when Renke passed it over, blurred and smeared before his sight. *For ten dollars and other valuable considerations, I, Edward Renke* . . . The signature tallied with that on the patent of title. Mark Malloy nodded and shoved the paper to Osgood. "Will the two of you sign as witnesses?"

When the thing was done, he folded the patent and the bill of sale together, put them into the inside pocket of his coat. There was a screech of chair legs now as Renke pushed back from the table, rising.

"Well, gents," the stranger said, "that was a damn quick game—but interesting!" His whole manner seemed changed, the desperate anxiety of a moment before had somehow been removed from him. He seemed to mind not at all the loss he'd taken.

Almost nonchalantly he turned and walked directly to that alley door which he had faced before with terror. Hand on the knob, though, he paused, turning back to seek out the face of Mark Malloy with a glance that seemed troubled.

"Say, mister," he blurted. "About that patent, I—" Then apparently he changed his mind, for breaking off he shrugged and muttered gruffly. "It don't matter. Forget it—forget I said anything!"

And, wrenching the knob, he stepped out into the night; the door was pulled firmly to, behind him.

For a long moment the three remaining looked after him, and at one another. Chris Henning shook his head. "There," he grunted, "goes a damn queer bird! What do you suppose was chewing him? What made him bust in here the way he did?"

"We'll probably never know," answered Malloy. He had gathered his winnings and he pushed back his chair, tiredly. "Much as I hate to break up the game—" he started to say.

That was as far as he got when a sudden cry went up from the darkness outside.

"Don't! *Don't!*" It was Renke's voice, rising to levels of mounting terror: "No—wait! It won't do any good, to kill me—" His answer was the shocking crash of a gun; running feet spurted on the cinders of the alley.

Chairs went toppling as the men within the card room reached their feet. Mark Malloy was the quickest to move; with one deft sweep he had his money off the table and was cramming it into a coat pocket as he headed for the door. He seized the knob, jerked the door open.

Outside, the alley lay black, between shouldering buildings and beneath the spangled arc of the starry sky overhead. But light from the open door spilled past him, and into this light the man named Renke came suddenly, running, his glinting eyes blank with fear. He seemed utterly to have forgotten the weapon in his own holster.

Behind him, the gun that had fired loosed a second shot on the echoes of the first—and, this time, found its target. For Renke stumbled, much as though he had stubbed his toe on the rutted ground. His head snapped back on bony shoulders; the sweat-stained Stetson tumbled off. And then Ed Renke went loose at all his joints and spilled down, as the bullet slammed him face forward into the dirt.

Mark Malloy had cleared the light-framed .38 revolver that he always wore in an underarm holster. Almost without thinking, or considering his own danger there, full in the lighted doorway, he snapped a bullet at the smeared after-image of yonder gunflash.

The assassin triggered back. Lead struck the wall not more than a foot from Malloy's silhouetted outline, as the roar of the two shots blended. But Malloy had the better luck. He heard a grunt of pain, the scrape of a boot, and the plain sound a heavy body made as it crumpled. His instinctive, hasty shot had found its mark.

It was all over as quickly as it began. Startled cries were building, belatedly, in the night silence of the cowtown as Malloy stepped into the alleyway, carrying a smoking gun.

Henning and Osgood came crowding after him and they moved to the fallen shape of Renke, whose shirt was blood-smeared now between the shoulder blades. Osgood leaned over him, feeling hastily for a pulse beat in the arteries of the throat.

The cattle buyer shook his head. "Dead," he grunted.

"I thought so," said Malloy, "from the way he fell. There was something damned final about it."

"What about the other? The one that killed him?"

"He's not making any noise." Still, Malloy kept his gun ready as he walked back there, cinders crunching underfoot, the two cowmen trailing.

The man he had shot was a black, shapeless lump against the dark earth, and unmoving. A sickness began to crawl inside Malloy as he dug a match from his waistcoat pocket; for all his fatalism, he hated death and feared it more than a little.

Under the flame of the match the upturned face leaped into sight. An ugly face, broad-cheeked, bearded. The whites of the eyes showed startlingly beneath half-closed lids; a dribble of blood ran from the sagging mouth.

"He won't do any more shootin' in dark alleys!" Bob Osgood muttered, roughly.

"Know him?" asked Malloy.

"Stranger to me," said Henning. Then the matchlight died and the night was blacker than ever.

Mark Malloy straightened, with a lift of his shoulders, as he glanced along the alley toward the nearing sound of running feet.

"Looks like the end of our poker game," he said. "Even if we don't know anything, I guess we had all better get ready to start answering questions. Here comes the law. . . ."

3

THE MARSHAL OF Saunderstown was one whose duties seldom called for anything more exacting than the jailing of a drunken cowpuncher, to keep him quiet until he sobered up. Such a thing as a double murder was foreign to the man's experience, and Mark Malloy knew in advance that he was bound to make heavy weather of it.

His first act, after perhaps ten minutes had been wasted in milling around in the alley and asking the same excited questions over and over again, was to demand the surrender of Malloy's gun. Handing it over with a shrug, the latter said, "Get some order here, can't you? Have the dead men carried inside where we can bolt the doors and then come down to cases. This is accomplishing nothing."

The lawman saw the sense of the suggestion. Some minutes later it had been done; with the excited crowd locked outside, he faced a grim knot of men beside the two bodies that had been stretched across poker tables in the big main room of the bar.

"So you shot 'em?" he demanded, looking at Malloy in high suspicion and flourishing the .38 revolver.

The gambler shook his head, patiently. "I shot that one," he said, pointing at the body of the man he had killed. "After he had murdered the other fellow."

"That's your story! Who were these two? For that matter, who are you, mister? All I know is I've seen you around town these last few days—put you down for a tinhorn!"

"You know Osgood and Henning," Malloy reminded him. "Why not find out what they can tell you?"

Big Bob Osgood was glad to give his version. He confirmed everything Malloy had said. "Renke had just stepped through the outside door when we heard him hollerin' bloody murder and a gun went off. We all started for the door. I was right behind Malloy and seen Renke go down, and then Malloy fired once and dropped the other. It all happened in a couple of seconds—and quicker thinking on Malloy's part than I could have done!"

The marshal looked at Chris Henning. "You agree to this?"

"I didn't get to the door in time to see the shootin'," the Cross Timbers man answered briefly. "But I don't think Malloy fired more than the one bullet."

"You could look at the loads," Malloy suggested.

The marshal flushed, not having thought of this himself. He checked the gun, and nodded. "One empty . . . Well, all right; Bob Osgood's word is O.K. with me. So one of them murdered the other—why? No identification on either one. You say the skinny guy's name was Renke?"

"That's what he told us," Osgood said. "The damnedest thing, how it happened. We'd none of us even seen him before. He busted in on a private game; and when we asked him if he wanted to play—"

"*You* asked him," Chris Henning corrected him. "I wanted nothing to do with him. He looked like a tramp, to me—a crazy one, at that."

Malloy said, "He was frightened—running from something. He seemed to know that if he walked through that door into the alley, he'd be going to his death. So when Osgood invited him to play he grabbed at the chance; merely as an excuse to stay where he was."

"That figures," the bartender on duty put in. He had been studying the gaunt face of the dead Renke. "I spotted this gent, Marshal, when he come in off the street—he seemed all worked up about something. First off he downed a couple of quick ones as fast as he could lift the glass and empty it. Then I noticed that he went over and took a post by the main door, where he could watch the street. I remember wondering just what the hell was wrong with the guy; but afterwards I got busy with other things and lost track of him."

Malloy looked at the marshal. "There you are! Somebody was chasing him, pushing him hard; and he led them into this town hoping for a chance to lose them."

"Them?" echoed the lawman, sharply.

"Why, there must have been two, at least. One that started into the saloon after him, and the other that had the alley exit covered."

The marshal favored him with a narrow, irritable scowl. "I guess you fancy yourself for quite a detective—figuring all this stuff up out of your own head!"

"I try to call the cards as I see them fall," Malloy answered coldly. He added: "What about it, tinbadge? You through asking questions? I'd like for you either to arrest me for murder—or give me back my gun and let me go to my room and get some sleep. I'm dead beat and on top of that, I got a headache."

Osgood said, as the lawman hesitated. "You got nothing on him, Henry. I'll vouch for Malloy. What he did was to stop a murderer, caught in the act. I'd say he deserves a medal, if anything."

It was this argument that finally settled the matter. The marshal, shrugging, passed Malloy's gun over to him. "All right!" he grunted, sourly. "We'll have to consider it closed, I reckon. Nothin' a man can do if strangers come sneaking into his town to settle their feuds. Now the city will just have to stand the expense of a buryin'. . . ."

Later, walking back through dark streets toward the hotel, Mark Malloy reflected that there was one thing which had not been mentioned—the homestead patent to Indian Springs. Surprising that neither Henning nor Osgood had brought it up; probably it had slipped their minds, in the excitement of the shooting and its aftermath.

But, so far as Mark Malloy could figure, that paper which rested now in the pocket of his coat had been the key to the whole business. He wasn't forgetting the eagerness with which Ed Renke had signed the deed away, or the way confidence seemed to return to him when the thing was done. Being rid of the paper, Renke had thought—wrongly—that he had thereby gained immunity from his enemies.

Malloy had kept his own mouth shut. He didn't care to advertise the face that he now held the patent for which Renke had been murdered—not when he judged that at least one of Renke's enemies must still be somewhere in the neighborhood. This realization made him watch the shadows, his stride lengthening at thought of the potential dynamite he had in his pocket.

Not that he wanted the paper, but neither did he like to be crowded. He preferred to sleep on this thing—his door locked and the .38 under the pillow. Afterwards, with head cleared and aching eyes rested, he would be better able to decide what he meant to do about it.

Mark Malloy walked over to the chair the doctor had pointed out and lowered himself into it. It faced the window; morning sunlight, streaming in with the fresh sage-tanged scent of the open ranges, stabbed at his eyes and he shifted uncomfortably, squinting against this.

"Hurting again?" remarked Doc Reading, drily. Stepping to the window, he drew the blind and Malloy settled into the chair, scowling.

"They sure as hell are. I thought they'd be all right this morning, but it's like somebody had poured sand in them. Well, you told me to come in and let you take a look. Here I am."

The medico waddled around behind Malloy, tilted the gambler's head back and pried open the lids, one by one, and not gently. Afterwards, he went to his desk and dropped into the creaking swivel chair.

He accepted the cigar Malloy offered him and as they both lit up their smokes he said, "It's like I thought—a bad conjunctivitis. I can give you some drops to make them feel better, but that won't stop your trouble. You got any spectacles?"

Malloy frowned sharply. "I will not wear glasses! I don't

need them. I can see as far and as clear as anybody, so you can forget about *that*."

The doctor shrugged. "Some men are too vain for their own good," he muttered. "Well, maybe you don't need 'em. The main trouble with you, fellow, is the way you been living. Too many all-night sessions by lamplight, in rooms full of cigar smoke and bad air. Too little exercise, too rich eatin'. It's no way for a man to live, friend."

Mark Malloy's scowl deepened. "Are you going to moralize with me, Doc? Try to reform me—make me over into a deacon or a grocery clerk or something?"

"Aw, hell!" said the doctor. "Why should I care how you use your life? Whatever you are, you're honest about it, Malloy; I respect that in any man, be he crook or preacher. No, it's your health I'm interested in—professionally. And all I'm saying is that the best thing you could do is take yourself a rest.

"Put those playing cards into your pocket for a month or two and forget about them. Better yet, buy yourself a bronc, throw a saddle on him, and head out into the hills. Get some fresh air in your lungs, instead of second-hand cigar smoke; and, incidentally, try using your eyes by daylight for a change, and on nothing smaller than a lava butte. Then come back and tell me if you don't feel a damn sight better for it than you do now!"

Mark Malloy stared at the medico during a long moment, aghast. The ash collapsed from the end of his cheroot and spilled down the front of his flowered waistcoat. With a sour grimace he brushed it off with his hand, took the cigar from his mouth and looked at it. Then he flipped the cigar, end for end, through the window, past the doctor's elbow.

"You're a fine lot of help!" he growled, coming to his feet. "What the devil would a man like me do wasting time in the hills?"

He left Doc Reading still sitting there—chair tilted back, cigar building a halo of smoke around his head; he went down the dingy hallway of the hotel's second story, with its drab yellow paper and its carpet worn through before each door. He was in his own room before he remembered he hadn't got the eye drops the doctor had promised him, and he was in no mood to go back for them just then.

He closed the door, crossed to the window for a look out across the roofs of Saunderstown and the tawny, breadloaf hills beyond. But only for an instant before he pulled back, squinting painfully in the strong morning light.

His coat hung on the back of a chair, by the bed. He looked at it a moment, and then on an impulse walked over and from a pocket brought forth the homestead patent and the bill of sale he had taken from Ed Renke. Seated on the edge of the bed he unfolded and studied them again, with a new interest.

"Well, and why not?" Mark Malloy said aloud.

Lips pursed beneath his neatly tailored mustache, he computed the miles to Hermit Flats. A couple of days should take him there. He had never been in that country, but it might be worth trailing over for a look at it. Perhaps old Doc Reading was right—maybe he did need a rest from card playing, and for reasons the doctor didn't know about. He had been going stale lately; crowding his luck. A change might do him real good.

"Somebody wants this paper," he reasoned, further. "They wanted it bad enough to murder Renke. And in that case, they ought to want it bad enough to buy it—at a good price, from the man who has brains enough to hold out and drive a hard bargain."

He nodded, liking the shape of his thoughts. "Why not?" he said again. "I can make this little vacation pay for itself. All I have to do is ride over to this Hermit Flats country, establish my ownership of the quarter section, and then wait to contact the party who wants to get ahold of it and dicker with him. Very simple!" But something made him add, "If I can manage not to collect a bullet in my own back before I'm finished dickering—"

Yes, there was that. But Mark Malloy was blessed with a serene confidence that did not much dwell on the prospects of failure; it was one of the basic tenets of his creed that

Mark Malloy could do anything another man could, and a bit more besides.

Still, it was something more than a gesture when he reached out, lifted his light-framed .38 from the gun-harness hanging underneath his coat on the chairback. It fit with a solid reassurance into the palm of his strong hand. . . .

4

AND SO IT was that Mark Malloy came onto Hermit Flats, on a sun-seared day when a hot wind scoured the bunch grass swells and whipped gritty dirt into the lowered face of a rider. These winds, he would learn, were familiar things here in certain seasons; for this was a high table country, open and dry. But a man grew used to the winds, and the bunch grass roots locked the thin soil in place so that it did not much blow away before the sweeping blasts.

Sleek cattle, fleshed out in the proper places, grazed the flats with their rumps turned to the wind, ignoring it. This range, which stretched wide and brown to the horizon at either side of the looping ribbon of stage trail, was the best of graze—sun-cured and rich; but it would be dry, except for the rains and the run-off from the blocky, timbered hills that lay along the northern rim of the slightly tilted table-land. And over there somewhere would be the Indian Springs place.

Thus reasoned Malloy, surveying the region through dust-rimmed eyes slitted against the gusts of the whipping wind. He was no cowman; but you didn't sit across the baize-topped tables from a long succession of sun-browned, range-shaped men and listen to their talk of weather and stock and market prices without accumulating, in time, a good store of second-hand information concerning the stockman's eternal problems and rewards. Winters, here, would be severe enough; but those hills yonder should give shelter to cattle in the worst of it. Yes, it should be a good cattle range—if the hoemen didn't come and grub out the bunch grass, and let the wind strip the soil of this tableland down to the bare

27

rock and leave it ruined and worthless. There was always
that possibility and that danger, these days when men
seemed to be moving westward in an increasing tide. . . .

They had a town up here, too—in fact, it boasted the dis-
tinction of a county seat. Mark Malloy approached it along
toward the middle of afternoon, seeing it first as a smear of
dancing sunlight reflected from weathered roofs and dust-
gray siding, and then taking the shape of buildings as his
bay gelding brought him gradually nearer.

Malloy was much more a connoisseur of towns than of the
range country that gave them life. He sized this one up
briefly, from long practice, looking first for the saloons, and
then for a hotel, a boarding house, a decent-looking lunchroom. These ran about standard, he judged, singlefooting
along the wide and rutted street with a spreading fan of
blown dust preceding him. The dust lifted, made a gray and
shifting screen across the face of the town and then scattered
as a cross current of heated air struck and whipped it away.

There was also a court house—a ramshackle, cupolaed
structure standing by itself at a cross-street corner. Malloy
registered this, for he would have business here. But now he
rode on past and angled his trail-weary bay toward the wide
doors and the splintered wooden ramp of a public livery
stable. It was with considerable pleasure that he stepped
from the saddle and turned his mount over to a barnman, to
be stripped down and put into a stall for a feed of grain.

The saddle was no second home to Malloy, and a long
trek like the one he had just completed took its toll. Heading
away from the stable along the hard-beaten path which
served as sidewalk, he moved with a stiffness in all his limbs
and body.

At the hotel he limped up the broad steps and into the
dark cavern of a lobby, where he signed the book and was
given a key to his room. He knew even before he opened the
door to it that it would resemble, in all details of furnishing,
every other cowtown hotel room he had slept in across half
a dozen states.

He had his shirt off and was struggling with a bootjack

when the kid came up with the clean water he'd ordered. Malloy threw him a half dollar and, in his stocking feet, padded over to the washstand. He grunted with pleasure at the strike of the cold water, sluicing the dust from his face and chest. It seemed to take some of the ache from a man's body, just to get the deeply engrained trail marks removed from it.

In the speckled mirror above the washbasin he inspected his face—reddened and peeling after three days' exposure to the full beat of the sun—and pulled down the lids for a look at the eyeballs. They were tired enough, from dust and wind and the daylong beat of sunlight on the trail ahead of him; but Doc Reading's advice had proved good and his abstension from the confining routine of his work had already relieved their condition considerably. Another week, perhaps, of the same treatment should have them back in shape again.

Well, he had made up his mind already that he would leave the cards alone entirely for the short time of his stay on Hermit Flats. He had no intention of staying long, and meanwhile he had another game, for other stakes, in mind. This, he thought, would likely command his whole attention.

He changed his clothes, removing the trail-soiled jeans he had been wearing and putting on again the cambric shirt and the tailored suit from his warbag, in which he felt more himself and less like some grubline-riding cowhand. The gun and underarm harness were strapped in place beneath the carefully contrived hang of the suitcoat, the light revolver checked and cleaned to remove any dust that might have drifted into the works. Then, with a supply of the cheroots newly placed in the pocket of the waistcoat, and the string tie and the set of his expensive gray broadbrim adjusted by the reflection of the mirror, Mark Malloy set forth from his room feeling more like himself than at any time in the recent past.

He went down through the old hotel building, crossed the dingy lobby and paused on the veranda to select a cheroot and get it lighted, with his usual meticulous observance that the match flame should set the weed to burning evenly. Putting the point of a shoulder against a roof support, he leaned

there casually smoking and observing the quiet, lazy life of
a summer afternoon in the town of Hermit Flats.

There was little enough stirring; but then, this was the
middle of the week. A cowpony standing hipshot at a tie-
rack along the street, a ranch wagon and team backed up to
a mercantile while supplies were loaded into the wagon box
—this was all thoroughly familiar. Mark Malloy considered
it for a moment, and then he swung down the hotel steps and
sauntered along the path toward the big, ramshackle building which housed the court room, sheriff's office, and other
local bureaus.

The county clerk was a baldish, officious little man who
thought himself considerably more important than those who
came with business, although he showed some respect for
this stranger because of the expensive cut of his clothing.
Malloy wasted no time on him. He drew the homestead
patent and the bill of sale from his coat pocket, spread them
out, and tossed them onto the desk in front of the clerk.
"I want this recorded," he said.

"Buying property on the Flats?" asked the clerk, as he
adjusted his glasses. "That's interesting. I hadn't heard of
anything changing hands hereabouts, and I generally hear
of such things before—" His voice choked off; his head gave
a convulsive jerk. Malloy saw the astonished widening of
the eyes riveted on the papers in his hands, and then the
clerk tore his stare from them and lifted it to the stranger's
face. "But—but this is—"

"It's a legal transfer of title to the Indian Springs homestead," Malloy prompted him, coldly. "There's Edward Renke's signature, on both the patent and the bill of sale. There's
my name, and the names of two witnesses. You have any
objection to entering it on the books?"

Confusion was a tide of color flowing up into the face of
the clerk. "Why—why, no," he stammered. "Of course not.
Only I—that is—" He showed his teeth in a sickly, nervous
grin, as Mark Malloy met his rush of words with a cold and
an uncompromising silence. "It's—just that it startled me
a little."

"No reason it should," said Malloy icily, "since it's none of your business. Your job is to enter it in the county ledger. Mind getting about it?"

When he left the court house ten minutes later, with his recording fee paid and the receipt in his pocket, Mark Malloy knew a considerable satisfaction. He had the county clerk pegged for a gossip, who could be counted on to advertise his possession of Indian Springs more effectively than he could have done for himself. This being the case, there remained little to do now but sit back and let the circles from his flung stone widen on the pool of public rumor.

So, having no desire for any further riding that day, he returned to the hotel and selected one of the sagging, cane-bottomed chairs that lined the gallery. The dusty wind had considerably abated. Malloy stretched out comfortably to enjoy his cigar and watch the slow shifting of afternoon light across the face of this town, to test the quiet pulse of its life.

It was as conspicuous a spot as he could have chosen, and as an hour drew out he began to be aware of attention focusing on him—of passersby turning to stare at the stranger, as they clumped in boots and spurs along the hard-packed pathway, and of the less-open observances of men half concealed in doors and windows of the town. He welcomed this as a token that his strategy was having its results; he had seen before how fast news could travel over one of these cowtown grapevines.

Suddenly, hoofbeats building to a sharp rhythm along the dust-blown street brought him erect in the chair. A single rider went flashing by him, heading north and quickly going from sight beyond the farthest buildings at the edge of town. Malloy had caught the Circle C brand on the rippling shoulder of the animal, and the intent, forward-leaning shape of the man quirting speed out of him. He watched the rider out of sight, and was settling back again into the chair when a voice in the hotel doorway brought his head around sharply.

"Well," said the man, in a slow, dry tone, "there goes word to Pitt Caslon, hell for leather. If that's what you've been waiting for, it looks as though you'll soon have action!"

He eased through the doorway, a long, loose-jointed figure
—not a cowman, to judge from the somber store suit that
hung on his body, and the soft, uncalloused hands with
which he tugged at his waistband, in what was obviously an
habitual gesture, to hitch his trousers higher on his gaunt
frame. He was clean shaven, pale of skin, with keen blue
eyes under a shelf of bushy dark brows. His soft, narrow-
brimmed black hat sat high on dark and crisply curling hair.
His nose was long, his mouth thin and quirked with a cynical
expression as he looked sidelong at the man in the porch
chair.

Malloy chose not to rise quite so easily to the conversa-
tional bait the stranger had thrown him, though there were
questions he could have asked about Pitt Caslon which, obviously, the other took for granted he knew. Instead, after a
first calm appraisal of the man, he simply turned his head
away and resumed his silent regard of the main street, letting the other decide whether he wanted to make another
try at starting talk.

The decision, however, was negative. With no further
word, the man went past him, down the steps, in a prowling,
loose-jointed stride. He didn't even look again at the stranger
who had rebuffed him, but went with an unconcerned air,
whistling a little, across the street and climbed the outside
stairs that angled toward a door and windows on the second
floor of the mercantile.

Malloy followed him with his eyes, wondering about the
man. There were letters painted on the windows of those
second-story rooms, he noted—a sign announcing them to be
the offices of one Frank Downing, Lawyer. For some minutes after the door closed behind his dark-clad figure, Malloy
toyed with his thoughts about Downing and wondered just
why the man had taken it on himself to speak.

And this Pitt Caslon . . . Well, the Circle C man was on
his way by now. Before too long, it looked as though Mark
Malloy could expect the first tangible results from the step-
by-step program he was following. And maybe a clue to the
meaning of the whole puzzling business.

So he continued to wait, and the afternoon dragged out to the golden hour before sunset, and a coolness touched the warm air. With the approach of evening the tempo of this town appeared to quicken a little; more life flowed through its streets. Once, a knot of three riders came in from the north road, saddle trappings ajingle, hoofs spurting up a rosy mist of street dust. Malloy watched them with abrupt interest, but none of the horses wore a Circle C brand and the riders passed the hotel with no glance at him. No Pitt Caslon among them, then.

At last Malloy rose from the chair when he had lazed away the afternoon, stretched a little, and found that much of the saddle stiffness had left him. Satisfied, he threw away the cigar he had been working on, went inside and ascended to his room to wash for dinner. There were already a few customers in the hotel dining room when he came in, hat in hand, and moved among the tables to one in a far corner where he had a view of the long room and of the tasseled archway into the lobby beyond. The food when it was brought to him had little to recommend it, but he was hungry after several days of trail rations and he ate uncritically.

He was finishing his slab of underdone beefsteak, and dusk was a blue dye staining the windows of the dining room, when Pitt Caslon came looking for him.

Malloy thought he would have known the man, even without the presence of the rider who had gone racing out of town to bring him. Caslon looked like a ranch owner, and an important one; even the film of dust on his clothing didn't conceal the good material from which it was made, or the cut of it. His boots were of good, soft leather, hand-stitched; his Stetson was an expensive one. The gunharness about his solid middle was of Mexican workmanship, carved and metal-studded. But above these surface things, there was that indefinable air about him of one who is used to giving orders and is impatient of their prompt fulfillment.

Now, standing in the doorway, he followed the gesture as the cowhand with him pointed out the stranger at the far table; he nodded curtly, and started directly toward Malloy

with a heavy and determined tread. The latter watched him
come, showing no interest, as he continued to work on the
remainder of his meal.

No, not a tall man, this Caslon—stocky, rather, and
square-built, with a solid set of the head on broad shoulders.
A grizzled, roached mustache emphasized the arrogant truculence of mouth and jaw. His greenish eyes were scowling now
as he halted at Malloy's table and dropped the knuckles
of a strong, bronzed fist on the edge of it. He said, without
preface, "So you've got it, have you?"

Mark Malloy drained the last of his coffee and used his
napkin, carefully, before he answered. Looking up at the
rancher, he chose his words as he spoke. "I could ask who you
are, who you think I am, and what it might be you're talking
about," he observed, pleasantly. "But it happens I favor direct speech, myself. Yes, Caslon, I've got it—right here." He
tapped the breast pocket of his coat, and then picked up a
fork and appeared to turn all attention on the slab of dried-
apple pie before him.

The table shook as the Circle C owner struck a blow with
his fist. "All right, damn it!" grunted Caslon. "I rode the
twenty miles here to talk this over, and we're gonna talk!"
He pulled back the chair across from Malloy, dropped into
it cuffing back the gray Stetson to the back of his blocky,
graying head.

Looking past the man, Malloy could see that every eye in
the half-filled dining room was trained upon that table, cov-
ertly or without disguise. He saw also that the dusty Circle
C rider had moved away from the tasseled doorway, edging
along the wall of the dining room until he had a clear and
unobstructed view of Malloy across the intervening tables.
The stranger checked this fact carefully, and then gave his
attention to the big man opposite.

"Talking suits me," he agreed. "Call your friend over and
we can make it a nice, three-sided conversation. More pleasant that way, maybe."

Caslon colored a little, but he shook his grizzled head.
"Dick Ford stays where he is," he said flatly. "What I've

got to say won't take long—but there's a few things first I want to hear out of you! Just who the hell are you, Malloy, and how did you get ahold of—the thing we're talking about?"

"You already know my name," the other pointed out, with a shrug. "Surely your stooge in the court house must have told you the rest of it—and in that case he told you that my title to Indian Springs is all properly signed and witnessed."

"I think you know that ain't what I meant! What's become of Ed Renke? Where did you run into him—and how did you ever talk him into parting with that deed?"

"Why, it wasn't hard at all," said Malloy, smiling a little, pleasantly. "Matter of fact, the three nine-spots in my hand did most of the talking. They outshouted Renke's two pair. It was like that." He nodded, still smiling. That was as much as he intended to tell of his encounter with Renke, and the latter's bloody finish. Some things would be better kept to himself.

For a moment, Pitt Caslon made no answer. His heavy jaw sagged in a look of blank incomprehension; then it clamped shut, his face grew darker with angry color. His lip curled. "A cheap, small-fry tinhorn!" he grunted hoarsely. "Is that all you are? And for a minute I come close to taking you serious!" His muddy stare slid across the immaculate, ornately dressed figure of the other; the scorn deepened in his face. "Yeah, I can see now you fit that part. But you better not try for one that's too big for you!"

Malloy said icily, "If you're finished, I'll ask you to excuse me. I've got other things to do besides sit here listening to insults!"

"You'll hear me out!" The Circle C owner leaned forward across the table, his voice hoarse, one thick forefinger punching the tablecloth to emphasize each word. "I want that patent to Indian Springs!"

"Very well. It's for sale."

"I didn't say nothing about buying it!"

The gambler's level stare held no expression. "First insults, and now threats? Are you threatening me, friend?"

"You?" Caslon's mouth writhed in contempt. "Why, I wouldn't waste my time. I'm just telling you that no damn tinhorn is gonna come onto Hermit Flats and hold me up. Don't try it, Malloy!"

"You're talking nonsense. I'm not aiming to hold anyone up, as you put it. I own a piece of property here; I haven't even seen it yet, but everything I've heard so far makes me think it ought to prove valuable, to the right party. I'm ready to do business."

"You'll do business with no one!" Pitt Caslon rose, gave his ultimatum, leaning forward across the table, greenish stare boring into Malloy's. "Indian Springs belongs to me! That turncoat Renke thought he could cheat me out of it, and maybe he rang you in on the deal without telling you the whole story. Well, that's your hard luck; anyway, what you won on crooked cards can't be too much of a loss to you.

"Because, I'm not paying a second time for that property —and nobody else is going to take it from under my nose. I'll have Renke's hide for his part in this; as for you—you'd better pull out of it now, before you get your own tail caught."

He straightened, finished in a curt whiplash of speech that carried across the stillness of the room: "I'm giving you just twelve hours. This time tomorrow morning a man will be around to look you up and get that patent. Unless you're a complete fool, you'll turn it over to him without any argument. Otherwise—I'll take it!"

5

Without waiting for an answer, the Circle C boss turned away and traveled down the room to the door, boot heels pounding the polished boards solidly, spurs chiming. The hand, Ford, caught his signal and silently fell in at his employer's back, pausing briefly for a last glance at the lone figure seated at the corner table before he brushed beneath the dangling tassels and vanished into the lobby.

For a long moment afterwards, utter stillness hung upon the room—a silence unbroken even by a clatter of dish or silverware.

The weight of every eye upon him was the clearest confirmation of a thing that Mark Malloy had already surmised —that this Pitt Caslon was a capable and dangerous man, with an important cattle ranch at his back, and with not much experience in having his demands put aside or lightly treated. His ultimatum was not bluff. Pitt Caslon did not have to bluff anyone, stranger or otherwise. He had his say, and possessed the power to back it.

Malloy rose, pushing back his chair, and at once eyes dropped before his stare and the silence broke as the diners resumed their meals. Unhurriedly, Malloy fished out money and tossed it onto the table, and then moved across the room to the same door through which the pair from Circle C had vanished.

He paused just within the lobby entrance, noting that it was empty. Caslon and his rider had left the hotel, and the sound of a couple of horses trotting away from the hitch-rack came through the hotel's open doorway to tell him the pair were already leaving town. Caslon was adhering to the

strict letter of his ultimatum, confident apparently that the
gambler would need no further urging to make him see the
light.

The low opinion which Caslon obviously held of him made
Malloy scowl a little, as he went briefly over that scene at
the table. He had been called a tinhorn before today, but the
word had never raised real anger in him until he heard it on
the Circle C owner's sneering lips. In this game he had dealt
himself into, however—a game that was beginning to appear
more complex and sinister with every throw of the cards—
he couldn't afford to let blind anger take hold of him. He
shrugged, with a characteristic movement, and only allowed
himself the bleak observation, *This gent thinks I'll scare
easy.* . . .

Crossing the lobby, he pushed through the half doors leading into the hotel bar to buy his customary after-dinner
drink. There were already a number of men in the line-up
and he had to wait a moment to get the bartender's eyes; he
was standing there when he caught the sound of a step immediately behind him and turned to see the lawyer, Downing,
at his elbow.

"You won't like the liquor here, friend Malloy," said
Downing, without preface. "They charge enough for it to be
good, but it isn't. Step over to my office, and let me pour
you one from my private stock. We can get acquainted."

Malloy considered the invitation, regarding the cynical
face of the lawyer coolly. Something prompted him to find
out what the man had on his mind, and the reason for his
strong interest in this newcomer to Hermit Flats. He said,
"Why, I never refuse good liquor. I don't mind trying yours."

"Fine!" Downing gestured. "It's just across the street. . . ."

They went out of the hotel building, down the broad
veranda steps and across the lamp-splashed darkness of the
street. The wind had died with nightfall's coming; the darkness was cool and still, its silence broken only by the normal
sounds of a small cowtown with the encircling rim of the encroaching flatlands drawn tautly about it in the summer
night.

The store building where Frank Downing had his offices was unlighted. Malloy let the other precede him up the outside stairs, which creaked dangerously beneath their combined weights. The lawyer used a key on the door, pushed it open and went into the room while Malloy waited a moment on the landing, studying the sights and sounds of the night. A match struck flame and the golden-yellow wash of an oil lamp spread through the office. Downing had a drawer of his desk unlocked and was setting out a bottle and glasses as the gambler eased through the doorway.

The office was bleakly furnished, with a scarred desk and a couple of sagging, leather-padded armchairs. Musty books filled a case above which the lawyer's diploma hung under glass. Cheap pictures of Lincoln and Washington were on either side of the window overlooking the street. A door yonder stood ajar on another room which would be Downing's living quarters: the end of an iron cot showed there. No carpet graced the floor, and the whole place had a smell of old timbers and mice and dust.

Downing was watching his visitor, a cynical twist in his thin lips as he saw the latter run a surveying glance over the room. "The outward symbol of a thriving legal practice," he said, and handed Malloy a filled glass. "Let's drink to it!"

It was good whiskey, all right, but Malloy declined a second shot with thanks. Downing pouring himself another one, corked the bottle and dropped it into the desk; he kneed the drawer shut as he pointed to a chair with the forefinger of the hand that held his glass. "Fewer broken springs in that one," he said. "Drag it up and make yourself at home."

He himself took a single sip from the refilled glass, then set it on the desk and moved to pull the blinds on the windows, one by one. Returning to the desk he hitched his loose-built shape to a seat at the edge of it.

Malloy, who had taken the proffered chair, leaned forward to extend his host a cheroot from the supply in his waistcoat pocket. Downing looked at it but only shook his head. "Don't use the weed, myself—and that looks too expensive to be worth saving for any of my clients. Thanks just the same."

Malloy returned the cigar to his pocket. "At the risk of seeming blunt," he said, "why did you bring me over here?"

"Why?" The keen blue eyes peered at him beneath the shelf of heavy brow. "It just looked as though you and I should know each other. You didn't appear to want to talk, this afternoon. But since that scene at the hotel, just now, I figured it would be to your own good if I made another try."

"You heard my little talk with Caslon?"

"Wasn't anybody in the building who didn't, the way the old boy was carrying on! You got him riled, friend. I hope you'll stand up to him."

Malloy regarded the other carefully. "And what is it to you?"

"Caslon ordered me out of town," Downing answered bluntly. "That was a couple of weeks ago and I'm still here. It's pleasant having another man show up who maybe isn't afraid of him, either."

The gambler looked around him, at the dingy room, and at the windows with their blinds shutting in the lamplight. "You're not afraid of him?" he echoed, pleasantly. "And yet you don't dare sit in your own office without the shades pulled—"

He saw the man's head jerk to that thrust, saw his keen blue stare harden and a muscle leap at the base of his jaw as he clamped it sharply. But Downing made no sharp answer; instead, he picked up his glass and drained it off before he spoke again. His voice was carefully controlled when he replied.

"I'm no gunman. All I've got to keep me alive here is caution—that, and the fact that Pitt Caslon has me marked down as nobody of any particular danger to him. Because, you see, this is Pitt Caslon's town. A man stays in Hermit Flats only if Circle C gives him permission."

"What about law? I saw a sheriff's office over at the court house today, but it seemed to be locked."

Downing sneered. "That court house is Pitt Caslon's private club; every man in the building works for him. And that goes double for Joe Legg. Our doughty sheriff makes it a point to look in the right direction and not see things he isn't supposed to. These last weeks, Caslon has had him busy out in the hills tracking down a bunch of small-fry outlaws who escaped from a chain gang over somewhere north of here. You can bet he won't get in the way when Pitt goes after you, Malloy."

He tossed the tumbler in one hand, so that it made a flickering pattern of reflected lamplight. "Yes, I'm harmless enough; but you, friend, are really stepping on his toes, and he'll give you the full treatment. Tomorrow morning, didn't he say? That's the deadline, and then he sends one of his men. In a case like yours, I wouldn't even be surprised if you'd draw Tony Balter himself."

"Who's Tony?"

"Just Caslon's official gunarm. He's crazy, and he's dangerous. I figured you should be warned. The more you know of this setup, the better chance you'll have."

Malloy thought this over. He could begin to see now the shape of the thing that was in Downing's mind. The lawyer was grooming him for the fight against Caslon; afraid himself to tackle his enemies, he would take this stranger and work on him and give him a buttering up, and send him into the arena little caring whether Malloy was killed or not, if he could perhaps put across a few blows from which Downing could benefit. This came clear enough and it added no stature to the man.

Frank Downing was cynical and crafty but he was still a failure—a broken-down, county-seat lawyer, going stale in these mouse-nibbled offices on the second floor of a cowtown mercantile. But he, in turn, had Malloy pegged for a thickheaded tinhorn gambler, who could be duped and played as a pawn in his own game against Pitt Caslon. And for the moment Malloy decided he would accept this role, because he needed information and the lawyer might be the very one to give it to him if he were kept unsuspecting.

Frowning, he said, "I'm beginning to think I got into something here that's a sight bigger than I counted on, when

I won this Indian Springs patent off of Ed Renke. It looked simple enough, coming here and offering it for sale to anybody who would give me a decent price for the land; this is dry range and if the Springs are what they sound like they ought to be worth something to the cattle ranchers hereabouts.

"But, the first man I run into is this loudmouth, Caslon, telling me that Renke's homestead belongs to him and that he means to take the deed without paying me a cent for it. That, I just don't understand."

"Why, it's really simple enough," Downing told him. "You see, Renke rode for Circle C once. Caslon and a neighbor, Garrett of the Star 7, were having a row about the Springs and when this range was thrown open to homesteading Caslon put his man on the ground and paid him regular wages just to sit there and prove it up for him before Garrett or any other rancher could get a chance. At the end of the five years, Renke was to sell his patent to Circle C for a cash settlement."

"That's been done plenty of times, in the cow country," remarked Malloy.

"Of course it has, but it's still illegal practice. Anyway, the five years passed and at the last minute, instead of carrying out his agreement with Caslon, Renke got a better offer from the Garretts and was about to close a deal with them when Caslon got wind what was going on. Caslon and Tony Balter broke the thing up; they put a bullet into Ben Garrett that practically killed him, and Renke barely managed to get out of town with his life, and with the homestead patent still in his pocket. That was two weeks ago."

"And ever since," Malloy finished, thinking it out, "Pitt Caslon has had men combing the trails, hunting for Renke to kill him and get that patent into his own hands. Is that it?"

The lawyer shrugged, hauled his loose-jointed frame off the edge of the desk. "Imagine for yourself," he said, with that sardonic twist of his thin mouth, "how he'd feel, having a total stranger show up with the patent and a bill of sale, register it in his own name, and then let it be known that he'll sell to the highest bidder? The man's fit to be tied!"

"Still," murmured the gambler, "it looks as though he had some excuse. According to his light, Renke double-crossed him. He'd hardly want to buy something he'd already paid for once."

Downing swung away with a snort of scorn. "Don't waste any sympathy on that range hog!" he said. "Caslon knew all along his arrangement with Renke was a violation of the homestead laws, but control of the Springs would help him squeeze every other rancher off the Flats. He thought he could count on loyalty, or fear—or both—to keep Renke to his end of the deal. And then the guy crossed him up."

A startling thought made the lawyer's glance narrow on Malloy, his dark brow dragging down. "You aren't soft-headed, are you? You aren't going to be talked or scared into giving up that patent tomorrow morning, without a fight?"

"I'll say what I'm going to do," replied Malloy, easing out of the chair, "tomorrow morning. Meanwhile, thanks for the drink. You're right—it was good stock!"

And on this unsatisfactory note, he nodded and turned abruptly to the door, leaving the lawyer scowling after him. But with hand on the knob, Mark Malloy halted for a final, blind thrust.

"By the way," he said, "one thing you forgot to mention, in that yarn you gave me: It was you—wasn't it?—who talked Renke into the idea of breaking his bargain with Circle C; it was you who arranged the deal between him and Garrett. That's how you fit into this—and that's the reason Caslon ordered you out of the country!"

The way the usually glib Downing started floundering, unable to manage a reply, was all the answer he needed. Chuckling a little at how his guess had rammed home, he slipped through the door and closed it behind him, and went down the creaking stairs in the full white flood of light from the rising moon. He thought, *Our talk didn't turn out quite the way friend Downing wanted.*

The village lay like a scatter of boxes, in that broad sweep of silver pouring across the flatlands from the eastern edge of the world. Mark Malloy stood a moment at the corner of the mercantile, beneath the light-edged squares that marked the lawyer's shaded office windows, and admired the quiet serenity of the night.

From farther along the street came the jangle of a mechanical piano, the ebb and flow of noisy voices. He heeled around, looked at the bright flare of light spilling from the garish front of the saloon; to Mark Malloy, who had spent most of his nights in one or another such place for a good many years now, the sight and sound of it held a lure that was especially strong after days of lonely trails and absence from bright lights and the company of other men. But he considered, and decided against that lure.

He was still bone tired from the saddle—despite his afternoon's rest, fatigue was crawling through him now. And tomorrow morning he would need to be fresh and ready for the next act of this drama.

So he turned his back on the saloon and its lights, and he sauntered through the moonlit street to the livery barn and had a look at his bay gelding, to see how the animal was faring. He talked to the barnman for a moment, and caught the covert interest with which the other studied this newcomer who had thrown his bombshell into the somnolent quiet of Hermit Flats. Afterwards, Mark Malloy returned along the pathway to the hotel, got his key at the desk and climbed the stairs.

Within ten minutes he was undressed and stretched upon the bed, his .38 revolver placed carefully beneath the hard pillow. He slept with the molten silver of the moonlight lying across the floor below his window—and with a chair tilted carefully beneath the handle of the door.

6

He awoke in the same position in which he had gone to sleep, to find gray of dawn pushing back the shadows in the dingy room. Drugged with sleep, he lay as he was for a moment, sorting out the jumbled impressions in his mind—until he remembered suddenly where he was and what had been promised for that morning. This drove all sleep from him and he came off the bed wondering just what time it was, and if the man Caslon was sending in from Circle C would keep his rendezvous hard on the appointed hour.

Going to the window, he looked out upon a calm, still morning that already held the heat of a newly risen sun. But as yet, shadows lay silver-dark in the street between the buildings, and the town gave up only the small sounds of early morning. Six o'clock, he thought. The deadline was less than an hour away.

When he had washed and dressed hurriedly, yet with all his usual care for the details of his personal appearance, Mark Malloy set to work packing his saddlebags. He carried these down to the lobby and dumped them just inside the door, and then walked over to the desk to turn in his key and settle with the clerk. A clatter of dishes and silverware came from the dining room.

The bucktoothed kid who worked around the hotel entered and Malloy called him over and tossed him a handful of silver. "Go down to the livery and fetch my horse up here. It's the bay gelding with the white stocking on the left foreleg. The man will tell you which rig is mine; there's for the feed bill, and a dollar for you. I'll be riding as soon as I've had some breakfast."

He saw the look the kid exchanged with the clerk behind the desk, and he couldn't miss the insolence of the mocking grin that spread slowly across the youngster's ugly face. "I win the bet!" the kid grunted, triumphantly. "I said you was yella. I said you'd run, all right!" He hurried away, jingling the money.

The clerk ducked his head and quickly busied himself with something or other at the pigeonhole mail rack, refusing to meet the glance Malloy shot at him. The latter scowled at his back for a moment, then turned on a heel and strode into the dining room.

A few townsmen were already at breakfast. Malloy took the same table he had had the night before and gave his order for ham and eggs and coffee to a bleached-out blonde waitress who eyed him knowingly. He caught interested stares from the other people in the room; not a one of them, he knew, but had heard of Pitt Caslon's ultimatum to this smooth-dressed stranger and were waiting for the rapidly approaching moment of the deadline.

Trying to ignore them, and to let no sign of uneasiness touch the surface, Mark Malloy gave himself to his meal while the morning light took on brightness and color and the first of the day's heat began to grow upon the morning air.

He was just finishing when the bucktoothed kid came bursting in, panting from his run, and loosed a crow of excitement in the uneasy silence. "You're a little too late, tinhorn! He's coming now!"

Malloy speared the last morsel of soggy ham, put it into his mouth and washed it down unhurriedly with the final swallow of coffee. Not another man in the room was eating, now; not another pair of eyes was looking anywhere but in the direction of the stranger's table. Slowly, Malloy pushed back his chair, rose, tossed his napkin into the wreckage of dirty dishes. He carefully replaced the chair under the table, and taking his hat from the wall peg he was putting it on as he headed for the lobby door.

The boy drew aside for him, that expectant leer pasted on his face. Malloy did not even look at him as he ducked beneath the tassels in the doorway; behind him, in the dining room, the silence broke apart the moment the stranger disappeared, every customer in the place joining in a sudden mad stampede for the door. They crowded through into the lobby as Malloy, pausing to stoop for his saddlebags, moved on to the veranda outside and there halted in sunlight at the top of the broad steps.

Below, his bay gelding stood at the hitch-rack where the bucktoothed kid had tied it, saddle and bridle in place. And yonder, across the wide street, a rider was swinging down from the back of another horse—a dusty blue roan, whose dark shoulder bore the sign of Pitt Caslon's Circle C.

From the hard-beaten path that ran in front of the hotel, Frank Downing looked up at Malloy. "Yes, friend," said the lawyer in his dry and cynical voice, "you get the full treatment. That's Tony Balter himself!"

Malloy flicked the lawyer with a glance and then lifted it again to the man across the street.

Tony Balter had made a quick tie and now he turned, with easy, graceful movement, and looked across toward the hotel. He saw at once the gambler standing alone at the edge of the steps and he guessed apparently that this was the one he wanted, for he focused his attention on Malloy's slim figure.

For a long instant no one moved; men were watching this scene, from the door and windows of the hotel, from the shadow of other buildings along the street, but there was no stir and no sound from any of them. And now, Tony Balter started walking forward.

He came with a kind of prowl, his knees bent, his head thrust forward, elbows crooked and spread out from his sides in a pose that turned his hands inward and close to the guns at his hips. For Tony Balter was that rare phenomenon, a genuine two-gun man. The guns rode low in thonged-down holsters, butts flaring wide from his slabby thighs. He came out of the shadow of yonder buildings now and full into the flow of the early sunlight, and Mark Malloy got his first clear look at Pitt Caslon's gundog.

A big man—tall and wide, with a hint of muscled power in the ease of his movements. A bullet-shaped head, the hair black and cropped close to the hard skull, eyes narrow and close set, mouth a mere gash of taut meanness in a wedge-shaped face. The tension of mouth and eyes—contrasting strangely with the relaxed smoothness of his movements—was the thing that betrayed Tony Balter.

The man was a highly strung instrument of nerves too tightly stretched, who kept himself under a strict discipline but couldn't hide the terrible strain of keyed-up energy barely leashed. Malloy found himself thinking, *This man is plain crazy!* But it wouldn't prevent Tony Balter being all the more dangerous, for that, and always on the thin edge of explosive destruction.

Tony Balter came to the edge of the pathway in front of the hotel, and stopped there, those fanatic eyes of his trained on the slim figure at the head of the steps. He called in a sharp whip-stroke of a voice, high-pitched and frayed by the inner tension that held the man: "Mark Malloy!"

And with the weight of many eyes upon him, the gambler nodded and said pleasantly, "That's my name." He dropped his saddlebags to the ground below him, and then came down the steps toward the gunman, without any haste. "I know who you are, and I know what you're here for," he continued. "I guess there's no use stalling about it." He was still moving forward like that as he lifted his right hand and started to reach toward the gap of his opened suitcoat.

It was a risky move, for Balter's reaction was just what he had expected. The gunman's right hand blurred downward and leaped up with a speed like the strike of a snake, the weapon from that tied-down holster filling it. But Malloy had counted on the man's iron control holding good even when the gunswift of his draw had been unleashed; and his gamble proved right.

For when Balter saw that the stranger had stopped his move in midair, right hand still inches away from that gap in his coat, he checked his own draw. The gun settled into line with Malloy's belly, its muzzle black and potent with danger; but at the last minute Balter held the thumb which trembled on the hammer flange. Eyes glittering and lips crawling with leashed fury, he glared at Mark Malloy.

And the latter smiled back at him, at the deadly gunpoint stabbed at his middle. "What's your trouble, friend?" he queried politely. "Nervous about something?"

"After this, when you start to go for a gun," the man snarled in his high-pitched voice, "finish it!"

"A gun?" The gambler lifted an eyebrow at the suggestion. "What are you talking about? I was just going to offer you a cigar. You smoke, don't you?"

"Don't give me that! There's a shoulder holster under your left arm."

"Why, yes. But it's empty."

Tony Balter didn't believe him. The man's eyes narrowed on the smiling face of the other; then, with the muzzle of his drawn gun, he reached out and flicked aside the lapel of Malloy's tailored suitcoat, revealing the gunharness strapped in place about his slim body. Malloy had told the truth; no weapon filled the clip holster, and when he saw this the gunman's face showed a quick astonishment.

"I said it was empty," murmured the stranger. "A gun can kill you, and I don't feel like getting killed this morning. I'd rather talk this business over with you, a bit. Now, can I offer you that cigar?"

And he finished the movement Balter had interrupted, taking one of the ever-present cheroots from his waistcoat pocket and presenting it to Pitt Caslon's gunman.

Tony Balter looked at the cigar, lip curling in scorn. "Them dinky things?" His hard left palm flashed, and struck the cheroot from Malloy's fingers, into the dust. With that same scornful sneer crawling on his narrow features, he looked into Malloy's eyes. "Caslon said I was to see a man. I sure as hell ain't seen any yet!"

The gambler had gone a little pale. He dropped the hand from which Balter had struck the cigar, and he said quietly, "I don't like your talk. I think you're only trying to force me to make some move to let you kill me. I won't do that."

"Why, you yella—" Balter spat, missing the toe of Mark Malloy's polished boot by a fraction of an inch. "A man that won't fight . . . I oughta use this on you anyway!" He hefted the revolver in his hand, so that the light of the high sun ran moltenly along its polished barrel. Then with a gesture of disgust he dropped it back into its holster, and stood with arms akimbo, scowling at the other man. "All right—I want that homestead title!"

Malloy appeared to hesitate. He swallowed, and said, "Is your boss going to pay me for it?"

"He ain't payin' you a cent, and that's final. Just hand it over all I'll pistol-whip you till you do!"

The stranger lifted his head and put a look around him— at the sun-struck buildings lining the quiet street, and the faces peering on this scene from doors and windows and from the veranda of the hotel at his back. He looked at his bay gelding, the way a man does at a means of escape which is only just out of reach. He faced Tony Balter again, and he said, "Isn't there any way—?"

"Hand it over!"

With a sigh of resignation, then, Mark Malloy reached left hand into his inside breast pocket and fumbled among papers that rustled there beneath his fingers. But when he withdrew the hand, what it held was the wicked, shining shape of a light-framed .38 revolver.

"All right, Tony!" he snapped, moving back a step as the weapon swung quickly on the gunman. "Don't touch your guns if you want to ride back to Circle C *in* the saddle, and not belly-down across it!"

A howl of rage broke from Tony Balter, mingling with the sighing release of breath in a dozen tightened throats among the onlookers of this scene. Balter made a convulsive movement and almost seemed ready to try for his weapons, but he checked himself in time and stood flatfooted, shoulders hunched forward, his face gone crimson with furious emotion."Get those hands up a little higher," Malloy suggested. "And now turn around and put your back to me!"

Nearly sobbing with fury, the gunman obeyed because

there was nothing else he could do. "A trick!" he screamed.
"A cheap, damn tinhorn trick! I shoulda been watchin' for
something like that!"

"Yes, you should," Malloy agreed. He switched the revolver from his left hand to his right and then, stepping
forward, lifted Tony Balter's guns out of leather, one after
the other, and tossed them aside so that they landed at the
feet of Frank Downing. "But you weren't, apparently. So
now, if you'll pick up those saddlebags yonder—"

"No!"

"—and just throw them on my bronc for me? Thank
you. . . ."

Tony Balter hadn't any choice, and with a groan of rage
he seized the leather pouches from the steps and flung them
up behind Malloy's saddle so heavily that the bay winced
and dodged aside as they struck, circling on its bridle reins.
Then the big man whirled on Malloy, his hands working, his
face a picture of frenzied hatred.

"Don't think you aren't gonna answer for this!" he
snarled. "You're not as damn clever as you maybe think!"

Malloy said, "You can take this message to Pitt Caslon,
if you will. Tell him, after giving the whole thing a good
deal of consideration, I can't see any reason for letting him
have the Indian Springs patent for nothing. It's hardly my
concern that he trusted the wrong man and gave Ed Renke
the chance to sell him out. If he wants to get that land, he
can bid for it now in the open market. And I'll be glad, any
time, to hear his price. Think you can remember all that?"

"I'll remember every damn thing that's happened here
this morning," Tony Balter promised darkly. "And you will,
too, before we're finished!"

"Very possibly," Malloy conceded. Still holding the revolver, he went to his bay gelding and took the reins, and
stepped up into the saddle. Looking over at the lawyer, who
stood in the path before the hotel veranda with Balter's
guns at his feet, he said, "I'll appreciate it if you don't let
him have those back until I'm out of sight."

Downing's pasty face was an interesting medley of expressions; but uppermost among them Malloy read surprise and amazement in this stranger—and a keen disappointment. "You should have killed him!" he muttered bitterly, thin lips twisted sardonically. "You got him with a trick but you let go of the advantage, and so you lost your chance!"

"That worries you, doesn't it?" said the gambler, drily. "You thought you were getting rid of him, and it didn't come off. Sorry, friend—but I don't like fishing for other men's roasted chestnuts!" He lifted the reins and the bay backed from the tie-pole. Nodding to Tony Balter, he added, "Tell your boss if he wants to make me an offer, I'll be at Indian Springs. About time, I think, that I took a look at this property everybody seems to want so bad. It may be, when I've looked it over, I'll have to up my price considerably. . . . See you, Tony!"

And, pulling away, he kicked the bay and sent it off along the sun-drenched street at a good clip, glad to put distance behind him. Not until the buildings of the town dropped into the middle distance and he was free upon the north trail, with the flat range stretching open around him, did he feel safe to return the .38 to its shoulder holster.

7

H<small>E HAD NO</small> illusions about Tony Balter. The man was dangerous, as a mad dog is dangerous; and the trick by which Malloy had managed to disarm him would leave the gunman with the fury of wounded pride and with a ravening hunger for vengeance. It meant that his own life would be in constant peril, as long as he remained here within reach of the Circle C killer's deadly weapons—and this independently, now, of Pitt Caslon's enmity.

Well, that was how it had to be, then. The encounter with Tony Balter couldn't have been sidestepped, and only by a trick could he have been sure of coming out ahead in that encounter unless he was willing to test himself against the other's professional gunspeed. So he didn't see where he might have done any differently.

It's just too bad, he thought, *that Balter had to turn out to be a madman!*

He rode without undue haste, though; telling himself with his usual gambler's fatalism that he could not spend his time skulking about and hiding in the shadows, just because there was a killer on his trail. He rode openly along the looping wagon trail, and the land was level enough so that he should have been able to spot another rider following him, against the horizon. Nothing showed, and this reassured him that Tony Balter was not in that great a hurry to come after him.

So he relaxed, forcing the burden of nervous tension from his body, and gave more notice to this land which was changing character somewhat as he came nearer to the northern fringe of hills.

The flat bunch grass range was breaking up before the

thrust of rocky spurs that ran out from the mass of the hills.
The trail turned eastward, skirting this region. On his left
now was timber, climbing by stages to the spear-tipped crests
that looked cool and shadowed from down here on the dusty
flatlands. The hot wind that had blown him into town yesterday, however, was stilled this morning; the dust lay close to
the earth and riding was not at all unpleasant.

Whenever the trail lifted to the hump of a rocky spur,
Malloy could get from this slight elevation a broader view
of the whole undulating flatlands, dun-colored, and spotted
with grazing cattle. Reflected sunlight from a ranch-house
window now and then made a brief smear of brightness. An
occasional breath down from the pine-topped ridges brought
the tangy sweetness of green needles, drawn by the warmth
of the sun's rays.

No outdoorsman by any preference of his own, Mark Malloy began to feel something of the stirring of enchantment
in this wide land. And then, near midmorning, he came at
last upon the homestead claim which had been all the reason
for his coming.

He reined in and looked it over carefully. He saw a crudely
constructed one-room cabin and leanto, squatting at the
foot of a slope grown over with brush and juniper and scrub
oak. There was a small corral and shed adjoining, but otherwise the place was without any kind of improvements. From
among a clump of igneous rock at the bottom of the hill,
water sang and runneled and flashed in the sunlight between
borders of heavy green moss, making a looping and lazy
course down the gentle dip of the slope in front of the homestead. This, then, would be the Indian Springs which held
such an important place in the ambitions of the ranchers of
Hermit Flats. And Mark Malloy could see immediately why,
in such dry country, this should be.

He rode forward, to dismount before the door of the shack.
It was substantially enough constructed to have stood for
five years, through winters which would not be too severe
under the shelter of the hills; its roof sagged but some attempt had been made to keep it tight, with patchings of

flattened tin cans. Ed Renke hadn't bothered trying to raise his own food; a small mountain of rusted tins cluttering the yard testified to this. Malloy stepped up onto the narrow stoop that fronted the cabin, and lifted the latch of the door.

He found the interior in not too bad condition. There was a trestle table, a couple of homemade chairs, an iron stove with pipe angling crookedly toward the ceiling. A window had oiled paper in lieu of glass for a pane. There was a packing case nailed to the wall, with shelves containing cans and sacks of food and with a door on rawhide hinges to keep out the packrats. In one corner, a wall bunk held straw ticking and tumbled blankets.

Mark Malloy considered these primitive details of housekeeping, and then crossing the room looked into the leanto beyond—a kind of storeroom, behind a gunnysack curtain, and lighted by another oiled-paper window. Both windows were hinged at the top, on rawhide; he opened and secured them by means of loops of baling wire to hooks fastened in the sloped ceiling. Clean air began to stir within the shack, cutting through the stale odors of old food and sweat and accumulated dust. It would, he decided, in a pinch prove at least livable.

He went outside again, and before remounting, stripped the saddlebags from his horse and toted them in and dropped them in a corner behind the door. In leather once more, he rode slowly across the swampy ground for a look at the place where his spring burbled musically from beneath the moss-hung pile of rocks.

It would be a never-failing source of water—one of the few precious supplies in this dry country. The man who owned this could do much with it; he could even, Malloy supposed, dam it in some way or deflect the direction of its run-off, thereby altering profoundly the fortunes of the lower range that depended on this water. Which was one reason the question of its ownership was such an important one.

And that was why, if he managed to hold out despite the threat of Pitt Caslon and the real danger of Tony Balter, he

stood a chance of collecting a nice sum from whoever finally
bought the quarter section from him.

He had a very dim notion as to the actual dimensions of
his property. A quarter section, he supposed, would be a
square running roughly half a mile on a side; but though he
had puzzled over the legal description in the patent he had
had little success interpreting it in terms of the actual lay of
hill and hollow. When the bay had drunk its satisfaction
from the clear spring. Malloy sent it splashing across and
rode eastward through tall brush and the shadows of slim
birch and trembling aspen, thinking perhaps to discover some
surveyor's plaque that would help him get his bearings.

Here, in contrast to the sun-smitten bunch grass graze below, there was dampness and dark shadow, the stirring of
small life among the underbrush, the whir of startled wings
in the branches overhead. Once a mule deer took fright at
his approach and went bounding away in a tawny flash,
through bands of light and shadow, its sharp hoofs soundless
in the rich leafy mold carpeting the earth.

He had threaded his way through these woods long enough
to be certain he must have overpassed the boundary of his
property, and was just about to rein the bay around and
strike off in a new course higher into the hills, when the
startled whicker of a horse somewhere to his right warned
of the near approach of another rider.

The first thought that struck him was of Tony Balter,
tracking him through this eerie silence; it was enough to
cause the .38 to slip from its holster and into his hand, as
with nerves strung taut he whipped a glance about him in
the cool shadows, hunting for sight or sound of movement.
The bay between his knees stamped restlessly in the leaf
mold, snorting and shaking out its mane. Mark Malloy muttered, "Easy!" and almost in the same instant caught the
stirring in a brush clump near at hand that brought him
sliding around in saddle with the revolver whipping level.

"All right, you!" he called warning, as the sound of his
gunhammer going back to full cock snapped sharply in the

quiet. "Start shooting if you're a mind to. Otherwise move out here where I can see you, or I'll start it myself!"

For a tense moment there was nothing. Malloy was about to throw out a second and final challenge, when the lurker in the brush decided suddenly to take heed; and as he waited with weapon ready and alert for action, a chestnut mare came shouldering through the brush and into the open, its rider ducking to clear the low-hanging branches of a birch sapling.

A surprised grunt escaped the gambler. The hand holding the .38 sagged a little, the need of the weapon forgotten, for this rider was no armed gunman. It was, in fact, not a man at all, though dressed in jeans and boots and a man's rough work shirt.

Malloy saw long-lashed blue eyes staring at him, frowning lips above a stubborn chin. The face was young and brown and delicately molded, framed by wind-blown shoulder-length curls black as a raven's wing and unconfined by the riding hat that was suspended by a strap from about the slender throat of the girl. Her figure was spare but strong, and well-shaped beneath the rough material of the red-checked shirt; the hands that held the reins were strong, too, and sun-browned—except that emotion now had them gripped tight until the knuckles bunched white beneath the skin.

Fright and anger were mingled also in her challenging stare, as she pulled her pony down and cried fiercely, "Go ahead and shoot! If I had a gun it would be a different story!"

Coloring a little, Malloy jerked back the revolver which he realized was still trained on her, and slid it hastily into the holster beneath his coat; but he still kept a hand on it, for he didn't know that this girl—whoever and whatever she might be—was alone. He peered beyond her, but could see no further sign of danger and returned his cold gaze to her face. "I don't like being spied on," he grunted. "And it seems better hereabouts not to take unnecessary chances."

"I'm sure you wouldn't take chances!" she retorted. "Your

kind never does. You always figure it's safer to kill, if there's any question about it."

"My kind? You've got me pegged already, have you?"

She tossed her head. "That's not difficult. Even if you weren't snooping on Star 7 range, where you don't belong, it would be easy to spot you—by your looks, everything about you." The girl went on fiercely, "You're no working cowhand, and you're no dude, though you dress like one. That leaves only one thing you can be."

Malloy prodded her: "And that—?"

"Why, you won't deny, will you, that you're some gun-slick Pitt Caslon has imported to take over Indian Springs and keep us Garretts from using it?" Her voice was scornful, bitter. "To take pay for a job like that—how low can a man get?"

Her words rang in the silence of the little glade, and for the good part of a minute Mark Malloy let them go unanswered as he stared at her angry face with an open admiration which he didn't bother to conceal. There was a certain humor in this situation and he must have let some hint of a smile touch his lips; for it lashed the girl to even greater anger.

"Laugh at me!" she cried. "Go right ahead! It must be amusing to know that, no matter what you do to other people, none of them have the power to stand up to you." She added. "You're even worse than that half-crazy Tony Balter. *He* kills because there's something horrible inside him that makes him do it—but at least, he doesn't mock at his victims!"

Quickly, Malloy ironed the amusement from his face. "Really, you've made a mistake," he said soberly, "and I think it's gone far enough. If you Garretts didn't live so far from town you'd probably have heard about me by now. You'd know I'm a long way from being a hired gun for Pitt Caslon."

"Then what are you?" she challenged.

"The new owner of Indian Springs. I got it from Ed Renke and the property's for sale to anybody who'll give me my

price for it. That could mean anyone—I'm not particular.
I'll talk business."

Her eyes narrowed, and disbelief was high in her. "Supposing that was true. What is your price?"

"I'd rather hear an offer. Frankly, what I'd like would be to get Caslon and you Garretts bidding against one another —you both seem to want the property, and want it bad, at least according to what I've seen and heard."

She was silent, studying him. The hot anger had cooled in her, but there wasn't any friendliness to replace it—only suspicion and a cold hostility; and Malloy gave her time to form her answer.

Finally the girl made a gesture that tossed her dark curls back across slim shoulders. "I'll tell my dad and see what he says," she promised briefly. "I'm Jean Garrett."

He touched his hatbrim, quickly. "The name is Malloy. Mark Malloy."

"I still think you're lying," she cut him off. "I think this is a trick of some kind. And after what has already happened, I have no idea my father will want to give you any money."

"That's up to him." Malloy's tone was indifferent. "He can ride over and look me up if he's interested."

He didn't know what he had said that made the girl catch at her lower lip with even, white teeth. But he got the answer to this when she replied, in a dead voice, "My father won't be riding anywhere—not ever. The doctor told us yesterday; the bullet Pitt Caslon put into him, that day in Downing's office, all but shattered his spine. Without an expensive operation, he'll never be able to walk again—"

"I'm sorry!" Malloy exclaimed, quickly. "Honestly! I didn't know it was like that. . . . But then, if it's all right, suppose I drop around to your place myself and talk this thing over with you both. Tomorrow, maybe?"

The girl studied him a moment longer, her regard cool and unfriendly. She said at last, curtly, "Maybe." And without more words she jerked the reins and kicked her pony with blunted spurs.

Mark Malloy sat and watched her ride away from him,

until she had gone from his sight into the sifting pattern of the trees. A good-looking girl, he thought, and one with spirit. But the kinds that he had met, in the vicissitudes of an occupation such as his, had taught Malloy small respect for women; and certainly, with the size of the thing he was bucking, there was no time for thinking about one now.

As he spoke to the bay and rode on, heading back toward the Indian Springs homestead, he dismissed dark-haired Jean Garrett completely from his mind. Or perhaps not quite completely. . . .

8

I t was well past noon before he returned to the cabin at the Springs, and in that time Malloy did considerable riding and covered that rough stretch of country thoroughly. He found a surveyor's corner stake and from this managed to deduce the shape of his property and trace its boundaries, up brush-choked ravines and across hills made almost impassable by patches of shin oak and thick spruce. Except for its water source, this homestead had not much clear value even as graze for cattle, and it would take a good deal of real labor to convert more than a portion of it to cultivation. Yet it had a kind of rugged beauty which Malloy was townsman enough to appreciate—and it did have the Springs, which made all the difference.

Coming back to his cabin in afternoon, he unsaddled the bay and turned it loose knowing it would not stray far from good grass and running water. He then went inside, built a fire in the stove and put together a meal from supplies in the packing-case cupboard. There was an odd charm about sitting all alone at table in this crude shack in the hills, eating food that he himself had cooked, listening to a silence broken only by the sounds of nature beyond the propped-open window.

Through the door he looked upon a world of sun and cool shadow; of blue sky and the stir of crowded tree-heads. A nut tree grew behind the shack, and the warm breeze along the slope shook down its fruit, now and then, to patter across the warm roof and plop to the steaming earth. And all this that he could see was his—registered on the county books in the name of Mark Malloy. An emotion he had never be-

fore experienced—pride of ownership in some small portion
of earth—began to stir faintly within him.

So touched by this was he that, having eaten, he removed
his coat, rolled up his sleeves, and fell to work cleaning up
after himself and also to making some stab at tidying up the
mess Ed Renke had left. He found a broom and got the
cabin swept out. He made up the bunk, using his own blankets—much as though he intended staying here for some
considerable time. He gathered fresh kindling for the wood-
box, and burned trash in the stove.

In all this he moved without haste, not being one familiar
with doing practical work of any sort with his hands; and
most of the afternoon had been consumed when he was done.
Malloy fetched a supply of clear, cold water from the
spring and used part of it to wash up from his labor. Afterwards, he took one of the crude chairs out onto the cabin's
front stoop and sat there enjoying a cigar and watching the
light change and fade as sunset came across the quiet land.

There was a row of white-bodied birches beside the spring;
their leaves twinkled in the last remaining day and then, as
the colors ebbed out of the sky, these turned to dim and
ghostly shapes, faintly visible against the encroaching night.
The run of the stream at their feet seemed almost to grow
louder, now. And from the brushy slope behind the cabin,
Mark Malloy heard the sudden, sweet call of a whippoorwill.

He caught his breath at the sound. The last time he had
heard a whippoorwill had been years ago, on his father's
farm in Nebraska. Now, head lifted, he listened for a repe-
tition of the cry, but none came. After a moment he took the
cigar from his mouth, pursed his lips and tried, as he had
often done so long ago, to imitate the sound of the bird and
deceive it into answering.

And sure enough, there it came, floating sweetly down
from the brushy hill. Strangely moved by remembered emotions of his boyhood, Malloy tried again. He waited a long
time before he heard the answer; it seemed closer than it
had before. He nodded to himself with pleasure and settled
back into the chair. Overhead, the sky had turned to blue

of a great richness, in which the evening star shone like a single gem set low above the western hills. The breeze was fresher now, with the coming of evening. Malloy looked upon the night, hardly breathing for fear of shattering this rare mood which it had brought to him.

It was then that the three shadowy figures came into sight, creeping around the corner of the shack.

Malloy saw them and they brought him out of his chair, the front legs of it crashing down as he groped for his gun and realized too late that he'd left it and the holster harness inside the building. He whirled, would have ducked in through the open doorway except for the warning voice that snapped harshly, "Hold it!"

Caught flatfooted, he straightened slowly, turning to face the intruders. Yes, there were three of them, vaguely visible in the dusk. And one of them said in a tone of startled bewilderment, "Hey! This guy ain't Renke!"

"Of course it ain't," said the one who had first spoken. "But what the hell! He answered the signal—"

Malloy understood, then. The mistake would have been almost humorous, except for the warning click of a gunsear in the hand of one of this trio; it prompted him to say, quickly, "Don't get nervous! I haven't got a gun on me." He added, "I didn't realize that whippoorwill cry was a signal, when I whistled to it."

"The devil you didn't!" said the one with the cocked sixshooter. "This is a trap of some kind. Where's Renke?"

"Not here," said Malloy. "And he won't be back. Are you friends of his?"

"Never mind who we are," said the one called Ike. "We want a look at you, bucko. Strike a match—but do it real careful!"

There was nothing to gain by refusing. Malloy thumbed a match from a pocket of his waistcoat and scraped it to flame against the wall. With it shining in his eyes, he couldn't tell much about his captors. He shook it out again quickly, saying, "If you don't mind, I've got reason for not liking to stand here with a light on me. It can be dangerous."

"Yeah," said Ike. "Maybe we feel the same way. . . .
Spud!" He jerked his head at one of the pair with him.
"Move inside and get the lamp burning, and we'll follow
you. I want to talk to this guy where I can watch his face,
and tell when he's lying!"

Spud was the suspicious one of the trio. He grumbled
something, and it was plainly with some reluctance that he
eased his gun off cock and then, still carrying the weapon,
moved past Malloy and shuffled into the dark cabin behind
him. No one spoke as he fumbled about in the dark, moving
like one who was thoroughly familiar with the place and
knew where to find the kerosene lamp and matches.

Presently a flame was struck and yellow lamplight steadied
as the glass chimney clinked into place. The one called Ike
said, "Better hang a blanket over the window." And when,
a moment later, Spud told him that this had been done, he
ordered his prisoner: "All right. Turn around and march in
ahead of me."

Malloy obeyed instructions to the letter, stepping carefully
and with hands lifted to shoulder level as he moved through
the doorway, into the room where Spud waited with lamplight pouring upward across the planes of a thin and bearded
face. The other pair clumped in behind him and he heard the
door bang shut. Only then did he turn, slowly, so that he
could confront all three of his captors.

They were an oddly assorted trio, strangely garbed. Only
two of them, he saw now, had guns, and neither of those
possessed shell belts or holsters to carry them in. They had
picked up odds and ends of range garb which more or less
fit, but all of them wore some garment or other that was
made of rough blue denim, bleached and badly frayed. Instead of boots they had clumsy, shapeless shoes. And while
their sun-dark faces were bearded, the hair on their heads
was short—hardly more than a feathery fringe topping the
bald skulls beneath.

"I know who you are, I guess," said Malloy briefly. "I
heard somewhere about the chain gang prisoners that were
on the loose, with the sheriff hunting for them."

Ike—the big one, with meaty shoulders and a face that was broad and tough-looking under its mask of beard stubble —scowled and made an impatient gesture. "All right, all right! We already know who *we* are; it's you we're curious about. And I reckon you can see we ain't going to be easy to monkey with, so talk fast and plain! Where's Renke?"

"He's gone," said Malloy. "I already told you that. He pulled stakes and left the country."

"And you're one of this Pitt Caslon's gunmen, I suppose?"

"Twice today, now, I've been called that—but I'm not! Caslon didn't put me on this land; if he could he'd throw me off, or plant me under it, one or the other. It happened I own this homestead, clear and legally."

Spud demanded, "You buy it from Renke?"

"My business!" Malloy added drily, "I didn't know you three came with the property; you certainly act as though you belonged! Maybe, since I've answered your questions, you'll oblige and answer one or two of mine."

"We ain't through askin' 'em yet," snarled the third of the fugitives, who hadn't spoken up until then. This was a runty, wizened figure—the one of the trio who had no gun. He said, "Who else is around here, besides you?"

"I don't know whether to tell you or leave you wondering," answered Malloy flatly. "If I said I was alone, you might decide to kill me and take over the place. As long as you don't know one way or the other, maybe you'll go easy."

The three exchanged glances that were swift and full of meaning to their prisoner. Malloy's jaw tightened as he read those looks and knew how close he had come to their real intentions. And then the leader, Ike, grinned at him, showing his teeth in what was obviously meant for a disarming and ingratiating smile.

"Aw, hell," the outlaw grunted, "we ain't wanting to kill anybody. We're a little suspicious, maybe, but who could blame us for that? We've been on the dodge ever since we jumped that guard, workin' on the county road north of here, and beat it into the brush. That's three weeks ago. In that time we been chased and hounded, and near cornered a number of times. We gone hungry, and we gone without sleep. Any man's apt to get scary under such circumstances."

"What do you want of me, then?"

Ike lifted a dirty palm, to rub it scraping across the stubble of beard that clouded his jaw. "Well, now, all we're asking is to be treated decent. We give Ed Renke the same chance and the guy was real nice to us. He got these here guns for us, and what spare clothes he could scrape together, and vittles—everything but broncs, which is what we need the most. He kept an eye on the sheriff and got us warning when the posses drew in too close to our hideout yonder." The outlaw jerked his head vaguely in the direction of the higher hills above the cabin. "We been laying mighty close since he disappeared a couple of weeks ago. When we seen somebody moving around down here this afternoon we figured of course Ed Renke was back. That's why we come in."

"And now you want me to take over the job where Renke dropped it—is that your idea?" Malloy shook his head, "No, thanks," he said coldly. "I've got a fight with Pitt Caslon on my hands, and too many other things to worry about, without spending my time acting as lookout man for a bunch of small-fry chain gangers on the dodge. It would be easier for me to run you in."

Big Ike's face dropped into a black scowl. "That ain't nice talk," he muttered. "And it ain't right smart, seein's it's us who have got the guns in our hands. But I don't really think you mean it. If you're bucking Circle C, it might be worth something to you to have us three around handy. Remember —this Sheriff Legg who's making it so damn hot for us is a Caslon man."

"I fight my own wars."

But the leader of the outlaws shook his head. "That just ain't sense, when you're buckin' anything the size of Caslon. No, pal, I think we better sit down and talk this business over."

"Out of the question," said Malloy, running a contemptuous look over this trio of scarecrows. "I don't trust you, and you'd have no reason to trust me. There's nothing to talk about."

"Sit down!"

Lamplight sheened from the barrel of the gun as Ike motioned with it toward the crude chair over beside the trestle table. Malloy followed the gesture, and the sight of his coat carefully hung on the back of the chair registered a thought in him: His holster and gun were underneath that coat, hidden by its folds. Maybe this would be his chance for a break.

He shrugged slightly, and under the menace of the drawn guns walked over to the chair, pulled it out from the table and eased into it. However, with the lamplight squarely upon him he could make no suspicious move, or try to reach the weapon that was so close now to his fingers.

Big Ike grinned at him, and passed a hand through the feathery crop of hair that stood on end atop his recently shaven skull. "Well, first of all," he said, "what do we need the most, boys?"

"Food!" responded the short one, promptly. Ike nodded agreement.

"You're right, Lefty," he said. "The last supplies Renke give us are about used up. You go back in the storeroom and see what you can scrape together quick."

"We need more shells for these smokepoles, too," Spud suggested, as Lefty headed for the door to the leanto.

Malloy told them, "There's a box of .45 cartridges on the shelf yonder, that Renke left. You're welcome to those. I can't use that caliber."

"That's right," said Ike, looking at him. "You must have a gun around here some place. Where would it be?"

"Find it!" growled the prisoner, suddenly wishing he had kept his mouth shut.

Ike's glance narrowed. "Maybe," he said with a harsh edge to his voice, "maybe, this guy called it right, Spud. Maybe he just ain't gonna work with us, at all. Seems a silly kind of attitude for him to take, under the cirmustances; but there it is."

Spud grunted, "In that case, we'd be wasting our time trying to treat him nice, the way we have. Wouldn't we?"

Out of the corner of his eye Malloy saw the man start toward him, moving at a prowl. He gathered himself in the chair, ready for a spring, not knowing what way this thing was going to go, but aware that it had suddenly got out of hand.

"Still and all," said Ike, on a note of real concern, "I'd hate to have to kill him. I've done some things in my time, but murder ain't been one of them."

Spud was somewhere in back of Malloy, now, out of the line of his sight. A sickness crawled through the prisoner at the thought of dying that way, a sixgun slug crashing into his skull perhaps, or the swipe of a revolver barrel doing the same trick. He fought the impulse to turn and look for Spud. He wondered, too, if this was the moment to make a desperate play to clear his own weapon from the holster slung beneath his coat on the chairback; it would amount to almost certain death.

"We'd be smarter to kill him," Spud was arguing, as he moved in behind the prisoner. "Leave him alive and he can set the law on our trail. Still, maybe I could be talked into changing my mind. That bay gelding he has running out there is one thing I could use. And there ought to be some money around. His kind, now, generally totes his cash in a belt next to his hide—"

Then Mark Malloy did move, but even as he came twisting out of the chair the pressure of Spud's gun dug hard against him and Spud's harsh voice grated, "Hold it, mister!" Red-rimmed eyes glittered wickedly close to his own, and as Malloy checked his movement under the danger of that muzzle digging at him, a dirty claw of a hand grabbed the front of his waistcoat and shirt, ripped them open with a single swipe and revealed the money belt strapped about his waist.

Spud vented a grunt of satisfaction at this discovery, but the near prospect of being robbed had made Malloy reckless of danger to his life. Making a quick twist sideways, he whipped a hand downward and struck the outlaw's gunwrist, turning the muzzle of the weapon from his body. Ike's yell of warning sounded just too late; next instant the prisoner had followed his sudden move with a chopping blow of his other fist directly against Spud's narrow head, felt the stab of spiky beard stubble and the solid hardness of bone beneath his knuckles.

The outlaw stumbled backward, his shapeless prison shoes scraping on the floor. Across the room, big Ike was shouting like crazy and trying to line up a shot at Malloy that would not endanger his friend. Dropping to his knees in order to make a smaller target, Mark Malloy pawed at his coat hanging on the chairback; but he was not able to reach the holster and gun beneath it, because just then a weight landed on his shoulders unexpectedly and bore him to the floor.

The uproar had brought the third outlaw, Lefty, out of the storeroom and, seeing the situation, he had thrown himself bodily on Malloy. They went down together, the chair toppling over on them both.

Sweaty stench engulfed Malloy, as he fought to throw the man from him. Lefty was a runt, with not much solid weight to him. The gambler managed to twist about and reach for a hold. A blow smashing against the side of the jaw nearly stunned him; but groping he felt the feathery slipperiness of the man's shaven head, slid his hand down the bearded face and got the heel of his palm beneath Lefty's chin. With all his strength he shoved upward.

Lefty's wind sawed loudly through gritted teeth. He clutched at his opponent but couldn't hold against that levering pressure that threatened to crack his neck. Suddenly he lost his grip on Malloy and was flung off him, bodily, the gambler's ruined shirt ripping from his back as the other got a handful of the cloth. But as Malloy lay there on his side, panting, the shadow of Spud fell across him and now Spud's right foot, in the heavy prison shoe, came arcing at his head.

He saw it barely in time to lift his arms and took the full force of the kick that way, sparing his face which would have been wrecked had it landed. Agony lanced through him. And it was desperation that pulled his arms away from his face and sent him reaching for that swinging leg. He got his hands on it, and he rolled away, and Spud with a bellow went off balance and toppled heavily across him.

At the same moment something hit the floor close to Malloy's ear and turning his head he saw it was Spud's sixgun, dropped as he fell. Freeing an arm he fumbled for it and got his fingers on the butt, and with the gun in his hand he squirmed free and rolled to his knees, one hand against the floor to steady himself as he swung the weapon up and caught the bulky figure of big Ike across its sights. "Drop your gun!" he panted, harshly.

It had all happened so quickly that the leader of the three had been caught flatfooted, staring at the sharp and swift struggle. He saw now that Malloy could kill him before he could bring his gun into line and work the trigger, and he didn't argue the point. He said, "Sure—sure!" and opening his fingers let the weapon fall.

Malloy still couldn't get to his feet—not quite yet. He was no rough-and-tumble fighter and this brush with Spud and Lefty had him exhausted, and drenched with sweat. He hunched there on his knees, clothes half torn from him, and held his captured gun steady with a tremendous effort as he gasped for wind and watched his three enemies through dark hair streaming into his face. He could feel a trickle of blood down his cheek where the skin had broken under the blow of a fist; there was blood on his forearm, too, where he had taken the punishment of Spud's vicious kick.

But he got up now, a little shakily, and pawing the hair out of his face he said, "All right, you two! On your feet— but stay back from me!"

The two men on the floor were rather less hurt than their captor. They climbed to their feet, sullen and scowling, and Malloy faced his prisoners by the flickering of the lamp on the table—which, by some lucky accident, hadn't been over- turned in the struggle.

"Well, what should I do with you?" he demanded harshly.

"You'll turn us over to the sheriff, I reckon," said big Ike, in a voice bitter with resignation. "I'd as soon you shot me. It'd be better dyin' than goin' back to that hell on the chain!"

"I suppose you were framed—all three of you!" Malloy's words were heavily weighted with sarcasm. The outlaw only shrugged.

"Why should we claim any such damn fool thing?" he grunted, shortly, and then all three went sullen and unspeaking.

It was stuffy in that cabin, with the door and the windows closed. Malloy moved over to the window, ripped down the blanket that had been hung across it. He felt stronger instantly, as the refreshing coolness from outside breathed into the room. He turned, considered again his three sullen prisoners.

"All right," said Malloy, and jerked his head toward the door. "You can go—but don't waste any time about it. And keep your hands off that bay gelding!"

Disbelief was ludicrous in the faces of the three; it took a moment for them to realize he was actually setting them loose. Then, dragging a deep breath, big Ike said, "Mister, after what we tried to do—"

"Skip it! I can't be bothered turning you in, even if I wanted to do Caslon's sheriff a favor. He'll probably get you sooner or later, anyway. . . . Here, wait a minute."

They had already turned toward the door, seizing the unexpected chance while it was theirs. As they hesitated, turning back, Malloy stooped and picked up the sack of canned goods Lefty had toted in from the storeroom. He tossed it to land with a thud at the feet of big Ike. "Take it along," he said, shortly.

"This, too." He jacked the shells from the gun he had captured from Spud, and tossed it over; the outlaw caught it, deftly. A swipe of Malloy's boot sent the weapon Ike had dropped skidding across the floor and the big man quickly scooped that up in one hand, the sack of foodstuffs in the other.

Mark Malloy had his .38 leveled and ready. "I'm a damn

fool to trust you three cutthroats," he said flatly. "Start moving before I change my mind."

Ike wanted to say something but at Malloy's uncompromising scowl he left it unspoken. He looked at the gun Malloy had returned to him, shoved it into the waistband of his denim prison trousers. Hefting the bag of supplies, he jerked his head at his companions. "We better do like he says," he muttered. "Let's get the hell out of here!"

When they had filed quickly through the door, Malloy followed them out and, closing it after him, stood there in the darkness listening to the sound of the three moving away, up the slope. They were lost to hearing, almost immediately; then there was again only the running of the spring, the voice of the night wind murmuring in treehead and brush, the early stars burning sharply in a deepening veil of sky overhead. The wind was cold against Malloy's bare body.

How many angles, he wondered, was this thing going to develop before he finished with it? He certainly hadn't suspected, when Ed Renke sat down to that poker table in a back room in a town a hundred miles from here, that as a result one Mark Malloy was going to find himself involved in a situation as complicated as this one.

He touched the stinging sore place on his cheek where the skin was broken, and found blood still oozing from the cut. He'd be lucky if he didn't have a scar to remember that trio of petty crooks.

Malloy was scowling at his thoughts, as he turned back inside to set water to heating on the stove and to clean up after the encounter which had interrupted his enjoyment of this evening's quiet beauty.

9

By MORNING, THOUGH, the hurt cheek had lost some of its soreness and after a careful examination in his shaving mirror Mark Malloy decided it was not likely to leave a scar, after all. This removed a considerable weight from his mind. As he shaved he was careful not to get soap into the wound; when his morning's stubble was removed and his face tingling to the towel and the whip of the razor he put a fresh strip of plaster over the hurt, combed down his damply curling hair, and proceeded to dress for a ride over to visit his neighbors—the Garretts of Star 7.

He took especial pains with this, observing the fact with a certain amusement at himself. If anything was sure it was that Jean Garrett would not be impressed to any extent by these efforts. If she took him for a gunman, she would not be apt to like a dude gunman any better.

Nevertheless, Malloy gave his clothes a good brushing and broke out a clean shirt from his saddlebags to replace the one that had been ruined in the fight last evening. His waistcoat had been sadly ripped, also, and he put it aside for a later attempt at mending. And, this being a social call, he decided in spite of the risk to leave his holster and gun behind. It was a gesture that might have some effect on the people at Star 7, making them more inclined to trust his good intentions and talk terms with him. He put a supply of cigars in the side pocket of the suitcoat, settled his broad-brimmed hat carefully and went out to his horse which he had already caught up and saddled.

The day was one to match the flawless night preceding it, the grass dew-sparkling, the sky deep blue with a kind of washed, clean look to it. The white-trunked birches by the spring shook their leaves against this sky, and Malloy looked at the sight and thought he'd never seen anything finer. As he got the reins and stirrup and swung up into leather, it occurred to him also that this vacation he was taking at the doctor's advice had already achieved its main purpose. His eyes were, so far as he could tell, completely cured. This was a most gratifying discovery. He was whistling a little, tunelessly, as he pulled away from the homestead and struck out on an easterly course along the lower hills, which he thought would take him to the neighboring Star 7 home ranch.

As it turned out, he had called it pretty accurately. He struck a trail through the woods and, following this, came out onto lower country and the bunch grass graze of the Flats. There were cattle, bearing the Star 7 burn. And eventually a flash of spinning windmill blades in the sun brought him into sight of the ranch itself—a somewhat run-down outfit, he thought; its buildings sound enough but needing paint. It was a homey-looking place, though. A windbreak of poplars had been set out behind the barns, and they were in full leaf. There was a stain of bright color near the porch of the house, too, which Mark Malloy saw was flowers. It would take considerable toting of water and careful tending to make flowers grow on this dry, windy tableland. Malloy thought the girl must be responsible.

The ranch looked deserted at the moment, the crew probably out tending to the endless summer chores of a cow ranch As his bay lifted dust at an easy jog along the road that led in from the big gate, Malloy watched for movement about the buildings but saw none except where a couple of horses were running in the barn corral. Once a man in a cook's apron came from the kitchen shack to empty a dishpan of slops, making a flat, slapping sound on the still air; he went back inside, the screen slamming behind him, and again there was silence.

But, then, as Malloy reined in uncertainly before the shadowed porch of the house, he saw that the place was not as deserted as he had thought. In the bright sunlight, he had failed to see the two people on the veranda who were staring at him silently, unmoving, and with open hostility. One was an old man, hair and skin seemingly as white as the pillow at his back. He was stretched out on an iron cot, so placed that his head was in shadow and the rest of him soaking up the warmth of the sun. He would, of course, be the crippled owner of Star 7. And the other person, standing beside the head of the cot, was his daughter Jean.

A little taken by surprise, Malloy shifted a bit in the saddle, raised a hand to hatbrim. "Good morning," he said pleasantly. "I'm making that call I spoke about. Any objections if I light down and join you?"

It was the girl who answered. "Yes, there are objections!" She left her father and advanced to the head of the steps, and she had an ugly-looking shotgun in her hands. She was dressed as he had seen her yesterday; she set the oiled stock of the double-snouted weapon competently against one hip, its business end covering the visitor with no uncertainty or wavering.

"I told you we didn't want to talk to you, mister. I also told you it would be a little different, next time, if I had a gun." She came down a couple of steps, the shotgun steady on its target. Sunlight and morning breeze stirred in her dark hair, finding a glint of sheen in it. "Now—pull out, gunhawk!"

Malloy tried not to show the very real uneasiness that squirmed through him, at his conviction that this girl would as soon as not let those double hammers fall. He assumed instead a look of hurt innocence, spreading his hands as he said, "You just won't be convinced, will you? I've said I was no gunman; today, I don't even have a gun on me. Look!"

He lifted the tails of his coat, briefly. The girl's look altered a little, lost something of its dogged certainty, as she saw that he had indeed spoken the truth. "You see, I'm harmless," Malloy persisted, pressing home this small advantage. "All I want is to discuss a business proposition, if there's any chance you people would be interested in dealing with

me for the property I have for sale. But we can't talk very
well like this."

He paused, and waited. It was the old man who answered,
in a moment while the girl seemed to be debating with herself. "All right. Come on up, then." His voice sounded very
tired, but not beaten. And as Jean Garrett turned to him,
ready to protest, he added shortly, "You can keep the gun
on him, if he makes you nervous. But not being armed, he
shouldn't give us any trouble."

The dark-haired girl made an angry gesture, but she didn't
argue. And Mark Malloy was already swinging down from
his horse, wrapping the reins about the handrail of the
veranda. The girl drew back as he mounted the steps. She
was very close to him as he moved past her; she smelled of
clean soap, he noticed, and not like the gambling house
women whose reek of cheap perfume had always nauseated
him. But her blue eyes were sharp with angry suspicion and
he didn't look at her, but went directly to the side of the
old man's cot and held out his hand. "The name is Malloy,
Mr. Garrett. I'm pleased to know you."

A rope-hardened hand joined his. The clasp was strong,
and the old man's face—so much like that of his daughter—
had the same stubbornness that showed in Jean Garrett's.
But the rancher had also a defeated tiredness, and when
Malloy released his hand it dropped limply to the blankets
of the cot. Malloy pegged him as a strong and independent
nature, suddenly cut down by the bullet which had laid him
out like this, paralyzed; it would have been enough to break
a lesser man.

Malloy said, earnestly, "I've heard about your—accident.
I'm very sorry."

The mouth of the man on the bed twisted, bitterly. "Accident!" he echoed, his voice harsh. "Well, I guess that's one
thing to call it!"

Jean Garrett said fiercely, "The accident is that he's still
alive at all. Pitt Caslon meant that bullet to kill him. It's a
wonder it didn't."

She had grounded her shotgun and put her shoulders

against a roof support, one booted foot cocked up behind her. Mark Malloy turned so that he could face both of these people. "I understand the shooting took place in town? In Frank Downing's law office?"

The old man nodded. "I was there dickering with Ed Renke to buy Indian Springs from him. Caslon got wind of it and came tearing in with that crazy Tony Balter at his back. There was only a couple of shots fired, and I took one of them; Renke, I guess, jumped out the window. Anyhow, he got away. And the last I remember of that lawyer, he was backed into the corner with his hands practically touching the ceiling and begging not to be killed. They tell me Downing's still pussyfooting around town, even though Caslon gave him orders to leave." The pain-tight mouth quirked. "He'll get his—and small loss to anybody!"

Malloy said, "Is there no way you can get action against Caslon, for what he's done to you? Maybe the sheriff is a friend of his, but if you got a warrant surely he'd have to serve it."

"What good would that do?" Garrett retorted. "When the judge is also sold out to Caslon, mind and body?"

The dark-haired girl made a gesture of impatience. "Oh, why argue with him, Dad?" she demanded. "This Malloy is a pretty good actor but he hasn't got me fooled. Pitt Caslon put him on that homestead and Caslon sent him here today."

"Your daughter's mistaken," Malloy told the old man quietly. "I don't know what it's going to take to prove to her that I'm just what I claim to be—the new legal owner of Indian Springs, who wants nothing else than to make the best kind of a deal I can to sell it, and get out of this country." He took the patent and bill of sale from his pocket, handed them to the rancher. "Here's my title," he added, "if that will help to make up your mind. You were anxious to buy the place, once. Well, you've still got your chance."

Ben Garrett read over the papers, his face expressionless. The man had blue eyes, very like his daughter's; his hair might have been the color of hers, too, at one time, but illness and the shock of paralysis had probably finished the work of aging him, of rendering him crumpled and old before his time. A humorless smile touched his seamed face now as he folded up the papers, handed them back to Malloy. "Two weeks ago, that property was worth ten thousand dollars to me. Now, I can't pay you a cent for it."

"Why not?"

"Because I haven't got the money." Garrett shook his head on the pillow. "There's a bottom to every barrel. And Star 7 isn't a wealthy spread. We've had Pitt Caslon for a neighbor too long—hogging the best range and all the water on the Flats, threatening us with gunplay if we dared to stand up to him for our rights. On Jean's account, I've had to go careful; there are no gunmen on my payroll—only three working cowhands and a cook with a game leg. With our herds being shoved farther and farther off the better graze, we've done good to keep from going broke.

"Five years ago, the Flats were opened to homesteading; but Pitt Caslon has seen to it that no nesters have come in and stayed long enough to prove up on their claims. Then, when he put his own rider on Indian Springs, to hold it for him, we knew we were doomed; because, if he controls that, he can take away from Star 7 and every other ranch the last available water we have been able to use, and so drive us off the Flats. And don't think that isn't what he's after!"

"But if you could buy the Springs?"

"That seemed out of the question, until three weeks ago when Downing came to me and said that for a healthy fee he would try to arrange it with Renke. It looked like my one chance, and I put up ten thousand cash—every cent I could scrape together, in the little time I had, hoping it would be enough to induce Renke to forget his terror of Circle C and sign over his homestead property to me instead of to his boss."

Mark Malloy frowned. "Ten thousand seems like a steep price. I assure you I'm not in this to gouge or hold anyone up. You could do business with me for a considerably smaller figure than that."

"Very kind of you!" the girl broke in with bitter sarcasm.

"Maybe next you'll tell us how we can raise the money—*any* money—now that we already owe our creditors ten thousand more than we're ever likely to pay back!"

"What?" The gambler's head jerked about as he stared at her angry face, and then again at the cripple on the bed. "Wait a minute! Are you trying to say that the money you raised to pay Ed Renke—"

"Is gone! Yes!" the girl finished the sentence for him, her voice rising. "What else have we been trying to tell you? Renke took it with him when he went through the window of Downing's office—and he's left us flat broke, with all that money to pay back, and now with Dad needing surgery that we can never hope to afford. Doesn't that explain why we aren't going to buy Indian Springs from you, or anyone else?

"It should answer all your other questions, too!" she went on, and there were tears of helpless fury in her blue eyes now. "And *that* was the reason Pitt Caslon sent you to see us, wasn't it? He wanted you to pump us, to find out just how broke we really are, and how much pressure it's going to take to finish us off!"

"For about the hundredth time," exclaimed Malloy, trying to hold on to his own temper, "I tell you I have nothing to do with Pitt Caslon."

"Stop lying!" The shotgun whipped up and its ugly snout was trained on him again; but this time her hands were trembling, her eyes blinded by hot and scorching tears. "You get out of here! Get off this ranch, you—you *spy*, before I—"

"Easy, girl!" said Ben Garrett, sharply. "This doesn't help anything." He added, suddenly and on a different tone, "Rider coming!"

Malloy turned quickly, ignoring the danger of the shotgun as he sought out the approaching horseman—a dark, unrecognizable shape, at this distance, trailing a sun-smitten plume of dust as he came toward the ranch gate along the narrow, twisting town road. He was making good time, as though some urgency were behind him. The three on the porch sensed this and fell silent, watching him come, their own tense words of a moment ago forgotten.

Then the rider's horse had drawn close enough for them to make it out to be a big, slab-bodied sorrel. Jean Garrett said quickly, "It's Nat," and some of the tension seemed to relax in her.

"Nat Huber," the old man explained briefly. "One of our riders. He went in to town early this morning, on business for me."

The horseman had turned in at the cross-bar gate now, and was coming up to the house. Mark Malloy stepped back a little, further into the shadow of the porch overhang, as the newcomer reined down and, groundhitching his dusty bronc beside Malloy's, came swinging up the steps at a run. He was a medium-sized man, not young, and with a red face and sun-faded hair. As he came onto the veranda he was already bursting into excited speech.

"Boss! You should have heard the talk in town. All about this hombre Jean run across yesterday—this Malloy. It looks like he told her the truth. He's a tinhorn gambler from somewhere; he's actually got the title to Indian Springs recorded at the county office. Probably a cheap crook, yet he stood up to Tony Balter on the street yesterday morning and took the guns off of him, without a shot being fired! Folks do say—" Nat Huber's tumbling words broke off short, then, as he caught sight of the stranger in the shadows.

Ben Garrett's mouth twisted in a slow smile. "This is Mark Malloy, Nat," he said, with humor.

The cowhand tried to make answer, but confusion and a sudden fear hinged his tongue and showed in his widened eyes. "Honest, I—I didn't mean—"

"Skip it," Malloy said shortly. "I've been called a tinhorn and a cheap crook before now, and I suppose I will be again. I can't go around killing men for that—even when I happen to be carrying a gun."

Old Ben Garrett looked over at his daughter, with a quizzical expression. "Well, Jean? What do you say about him now? Is he what he claims to be—or do you still insist he's a hired gun for Circle C?"

The girl's consternation was as great as that of the red-faced puncher. She had lowered her shotgun to the porch floor, and she stood facing Malloy with a look of utter bemusement, as though unable to find any words. The gambler, with no desire to embarrass her, stepped forward quickly.

"I could hardly blame anyone for misreading the sign, things being as mixed up as they are. Personally, I'm ready to forget any hasty words that may have been said."

Her glance wavered, her parted lips quivering a little. But then she recovered herself and her chin lifted, that stubborn thrust coming into it once more.

Jean Garrett said, "I don't know that I'm ready to forget. If I've made a mistake, I suppose some day I'll have to apologize. But right now I still don't like the looks of this. I still can't picture anybody like you standing up to Tony Balter. It would be easier to believe the whole thing was deliberately staged."

"Oh, now, Jean!" Her father sounded angry. But Malloy was cool enough.

"It doesn't matter—let her think what she likes. Sooner or later, we can hope that things will be ironed out and then we'll all know where we stand." He added, "I'm glad to have talked with you, Garrett. I wish you luck. I'm sorry we couldn't do business."

"And what becomes of Indian Springs? You'll be letting Pitt Caslon have them, I suppose, after all—either on your own terms, or on his."

"I don't know," Malloy admitted, his frown troubled. "I don't really know. . . ."

On that uncertain note, the conversation ended.

10

It was more of the fine weather, as clear as the tone of a bronze bell. Malloy rode high in saddle, filling his lungs with the winey air that carried pine scent off the hills, and continuing to wonder at himself. He had never before spent so many hours on horseback, or thought that he would want to. But though his body held soreness, he had slept well and his appetite was above reproach; this change of pace must be doing him good.

Right now, his thouhts were largely occupied with the scene just concluded back yonder at the Garrett place. He had learned, however, that it was wise for a man in these hills to keep his senses constantly on the alert; and so it was that when a horseman crossed an open space among the trees ahead of him, he caught the brief flash of movement and check-reined in quick alarm.

Though he waited there was no further movement; and this seemed warning enough. The rider must be deliberately trying to keep out of sight—which could mean only one thing, to Malloy's reckoning. He was a Caslon spy.

Mouth gone stern, Malloy considered this while he ran a long glance over the green face of the hills that pocketed him. He had no intention of riding into an ambush, if that was Caslon's purpose. To avoid it, he made a quick choice and, pulling out of the trail, sent his gelding at a hill rising opposite the place where he had seen the horseman.

He crossed this ridge, and saw stretched ahead of him the wide expanse of the Flats, tawny in summer's heat, with the occasional pillar of a dust devil moving slowly across it, and the tiny red shapes of grazing cattle. The broad view was cut off by other ridges that lifted between, as he descended into the ravine beyond. He took the downslope at an angle, followed the ravine until it ran out against the flank of an outjutting slope, and climbed again.

Cresting this ridge, he jerked rein with a sudden exclamation and pulled his gelding into the shelter of a juniper. On a neighboring ridge a second rider was silhouetted plainly against the sky, as he twisted slowly for a sweeping survey of the ground that lay below him. The sun flashed from the lenses of binoculars in his hands.

Malloy cursed in alarms. Caslon meant business! Obviously this was a Circle C rider, warned by the first that their quarry had quit the trail and broken in his direction. No telling how many others there might be, sent out to waylay the troublesome stranger somewhere in the empty hills and dispose of him.

Now the horseman on yonder ridge had moved on out of sight, leaving no sign that he had ever been. A moment of panic touched Malloy at the thought of unseen enemies closing in on him, in hills that they knew thoroughly but which were utterly foreign to himself. But he called his poker-playing discipline into use and, forcing a control on himself, sent the gelding ahead.

With Caslon's riders on either flank, he had no choice but to follow this ridge, dropping down a little below its crest to let it shield him from their binoculars. The going was treacherous, steep-slanting. Part of the time he could hug the shadow of sidehill growth, but whenever the sun's warm hand touched him he winced, knowing he had lost this protection. He found himself throwing wild glances over his shoulder, hunting for Caslon's riders but discovering only the motionless stillness of the hills.

Then the ridge he had followed played out against the flank of a barren spine of rock and he would have to cross this, putting himself plainly against the sky to do so. Sweat that wasn't entirely due to the high sun broke out on him; he felt it trickle coldly across his ribs, tickling a shiver through him. Desperately, he kicked the bay gelding forward.

He had almost cleared that open stretch when the lash of a rifle sounded upon the high air.

It was a snapshot and too far away for accuracy, but rock chips leaped and the gelding nearly stumbled at Malloy's quick pull on the leathers. It scrambled for footing, took him the remaining distance to drop safely past the knife-edge beyond; but not before he heard, thin and sharp, a shout behind him.

They had him spotted, now, and now they could close in, riding the rims to herd him in any direction they wanted until they were ready to finish him off. And he, caught like this without any sort of weapon!

Malloy raced ahead, trying no longer for secrecy but only to put as much distance as possible behind himself, and to find a way down off these ridges. For the hundredth time he wished he knew this country; as it was, plunging blindly ahead, he might at any moment run into a trap. . . . Pulling rein, presently, he swung back for a look.

He still could not see his hunters, but he knew they were there—behind him, perhaps moving in along any of these ridges that shouldered his own. He squared around again, peered ahead over the treetops toward lower ground.

Almost directly below him, where a draw debouched from between sheltering, wooded hills, stood a good-sized cattle spread. Though distant, and foreshortened at this angle of vision, the sparkling air rendered its buildings as distinct and sharp as images seen through the wrong end of a telescope. They might offer him shelter, if he could manage to reach them. Unless

His heart sank. This was not one of the numerous small spreads that spotted the Flats and the rim of the foothills. It had too many buildings, and they were too large; the main house even boasted a double story. Malloy knew there were only a couple of large-sized ranches in the district— and this wasn't Garrett's Star 7.

So he'd let himself be tolled straight into Pitt Caslon's own front yard!

It put him in a bad dilemma. He couldn't face about, and

he could hardly ride down there toward Circle C. . . . But then his saving, native audacity returned to him and he saw that this, in fact, was the very thing he would have to do. Brazen nerve and bluff might yet win him this hand, just as it had won for him countless times before, over countless card-littered gaming tables.

"Let's go!" he told the bay gelding, and shook out the reins to send the animal forward.

Coming down off the hills, he soon found a dim saddle trail that pointed toward the ranch, and this saved him time. In a few minutes ground leveled out, the last fringe of pine and aspen fell back, and he was crossing a deep-grassed park with the buildings and corrals of Circle C opening before him. He made for these, without hurry; no sign of tightening nerves showed itself in his calm, expressionless features as he carefully studied the layout of the place.

Unlike the hard-pressed Garretts, he judged, Pitt Caslon was running a full crew—and prospering. A big new barn was going up, its unpainted lumber shining cleanly in the sun. There were two bunk shacks, and the sprawling corrals with their hayracks covered a lot of space. The saddle stock running in the pens looked good to Malloy's eyes, and he saw it was all carefully branded in the Circle C iron. Caslon would be one to take arrogant pride in his accomplishments; he would want his brand on everything he owned, to be seen and recognized and respected by the lesser breed of men.

At an open-faced blacksmith shed, a saddler which did not wear the Caslon brand was being shoed. The strokes of the hammer reached Malloy before he came around into view of the place and saw the brawny cowhand working, and the other pair of men who squatted on their heels to watch. He recognized one of these immediately, by his stocky and squarebuilt shape; an instant later, happening to turn his head, Pitt Caslon sighted the newcomer and at once he was coming to his feet with awkward haste.

The Circle C boss strode into the open as Malloy halted; his head was shot forward, mouth set hard beneath the roached mustache, greenish eyes narrowed and dangerous with suspicion. "You?"

Malloy nodded pleasantly. "Since we're neighbors, I thought it was only fitting that I paid a visit."

"Neighbors!" echoed Caslon, and spat into the dirt. He added: "You never come here of your own accord. You wouldn't of had the nerve!"

The other rested a forearm across the saddle swell, smiled a little at the man on the ground. "Why not?" he murmured. "I thought maybe you'd be ready to talk business. You must have learned by this time that I'm not going to be bluffed out, Caslon!"

Pitt Caslon was not looking at him, however. Something had drawn his stare to a point beyond Malloy and the latter, for all the riskiness of taking his own eyes off the cattleman, couldn't resist the urge to look. He twisted about, flung a quick glance back and at once saw what had caught the other's eye.

The dark, moving figures of horsemen had broken into sight, at scattered points along that timber fringe where the meadow joined the skirt of the hills. Malloy counted three of them, spurring in to converge upon the ranch; and they were coming fast.

"So *that* explains why you rode down here!" Pitt Caslon exclaimed. "You must be a bigger fool than I took you for, Malloy!"

He didn't answer. The man whose horse had just been re-shod was walking out from under the shadow of the black-smith shed, leading the animal, and Malloy's attention switched to him.

A tall, reedy individual, this one, with shoulders considerably rounded, and a ferocious black mustache whose effect was spoiled by a constant expression of puzzled concentration that rode his frowning, squinted eyes. His clothing was trail stained, his body drooping with tiredness. The silver star pinned to his shirt front sagged against his thin chest.

A quick and irrational surge of hope went through Malloy, even while the drum of racing hoofs beat echoes off the hillslopes, and those racing horsemen came pounding in toward the ranch. "Sheriff Legg, isn't it?" he observed. "This is fortunate, indeed! You're the very man I want to see."

"Yeah?" The lawman peered at him with his questioning scowl. Pitt Caslon seemed a bit less smug, now, a bit less sure of himself; obviously he was wondering what Malloy thought he might be up to. The sheriff said, "So what can I do for you?"

"I just ran into trouble," Malloy told him. "Somebody who took a shot at me with a rifle—meant to kill me, I figure. As sheriff of this county, you should know what can happen to a rider minding his own business on the trails. It's your place to do something about it."

"Are you filing charges?" Joe Legg wanted to know, that same frown of puzzled concentration on him. "Could you identify whoever it was used the rifle?"

"Why, as for that—"

Malloy turned his head, watching the three riders who were now clattering into the ranchyard, rounding the corrals. They all at once had pulled rein as they sighted Malloy and Caslon and the sheriff, and a quick film of dust lifted and was whisked away by the ground breeze. Through this, Malloy took a long look at the trio.

Dick Ford, and Tony Balter, and a third that he didn't know, although he too rode a Circle C horse. All three mounts were lathered, and there was a long gun in scabbard slung to each of their saddles.

"As for identifying anyone," Malloy said, turning back to the sheriff, "it's yes and no. I might come pretty close. I might be able to lay my hand on a saddle gun that had been fired within the last quarter hour. Of course, that wouldn't be jury evidence. . . ."

Legg shook his head thoughtfully. "No," he agreed, "it probably wouldn't. The law would say—"

"You fool!" Pitt Caslon spat at him. "Can't you get it into your thick head that you're bein' made fun of? This is him—this is Malloy, himself!"

The meaning of it all seemed to take a moment, sinking in.

Legg shot a startled look at the Circle C owner, and then he turned his head and studied the three riders who had just come out of the hills; he saw the thunderous scowl on Tony Balter's mean face, and the way Tony's hand was rubbing the rifle stock that jutted up from beneath his knees. All at once his slow wits made connection, and a flush began and burned its way up into his florid, bony features.

"Hell!" he exclaimed apologetically. "I didn't know, Caslon! I didn't know he was talkin' about—"

"I'm talking about your duty as an officer of the law!" Malloy corrected him sternly. "What do you use that badge for anyway—just to pin up your galluses?"

"Now, you wait a minute!" cried Legg, stung by the taunting. Malloy went right on, however, not giving him a chance to break in.

"A fine thing, that a man can't ride the trails on peaceable business without some dirty backshooter going to work on him. If it's robbery he was after, he wasted his lead; at least, I have sense enough to put my valuables in a safe place, before risking my neck in strange country!" He added, looking squarely at Pitt Caslon, "And I mean *all* my valuables!"

Caslon's eyes flickered as he took this in. Sheriff Legg, meanwhile, was opening his mouth and closing it again, making unintelligible noises. Yonder, Tony Balter stirred in the saddle and he said harshly, "All right, Malloy! If you're finished with all your loudmouthing, I'm ready to take up what you done to me in town yesterday!"

"No, Tony!"

The sharp words caught Balter up, turned him on his employer with an angry cry. "Boss, you promised me—"

"Not this time!" Caslon's voice was sour with admitted defeat. "Malloy, if you know when you're plain, damn lucky you'll get that bronc headed away from here—fast!"

A high, unbearable tension eased within Mark Malloy, then; the game had been tight but his bluff had won. Every man, however spineless, has his pride, and the caustic thrusts at Joe Legg had plainly stung some deeply buried instinct to self-respect within Pitt Caslon's sheriff. The Circle C boss knew this, and knew he couldn't risk violence, with Legg in such a mood.

Obviously, too, he had believed Malloy's broad hint that the Indian Spring patent was hidden and beyond his reach, where murder wouldn't get it for him. As a matter of fact, the paper was even then in Malloy's coat pocket. But at the first opportunity, he promised himself he would remedy that carelessness. . . .

Malloy drew a long breath. "Heading for town, sheriff?" he suggested. "If you are I'll sideride you."

In indecision, Legg glanced at the Circle C owner, but Caslon only shrugged and looked away. This was a dismissal and, after another moment's hesitation, the sheriff stepped around to the side of his horse and fumbled for the stirrup, lifted his beanpole length into saddle. Malloy swung his bay gelding about, to put it alongside the sheriff's spotted gray.

"Boss—!"

The anguished cry exploded from Tony Balter. Insane and raging anger shone in Tony's close-set eyes, struggling there with the fear and respect he held for Pitt Caslon's wishes. When his appeal got no answer, the gunman somehow managed to hold himself in check, tight lips working. But the look of him was enough to put a tingling of uncanny dread down Mark Malloy's spine.

Then Pitt Caslon himself spoke up, unexpectedly, and his voice was bitter. "What's your price, hombre?"

"For Indian Springs?" Malloy whipped a startled glance at him. "You don't mean you're giving in?"

Caslon's stare was wooden. "Just give me an answer. Name your figure!"

Suddenly, Mark Malloy knew this was a real victory; through nerve and bluff he had won from the big man a virtual admission that he'd underestimated his opponent. In that instant Malloy felt sure, if the sum he asked were not too outrageous for the man's battered ego to accept, Caslon would have chosen to pay rather than continue the fight.

But something in Malloy had changed, too, since the start

of this business; a stubbornness had settled in him, that made him shake his head now and tell Pitt Caslon, flatly, "It's too bad you didn't feel like talking terms a couple of evenings ago, mister—when I was in the mood. Since then, I've seen this Indian Springs property, and I've kind of taken a liking to it. Maybe now I don't want to sell at all. Maybe I'll keep the place myself."

Pitt Caslon's head jerked, as though he had been struck. "You—you . . ." he choked, and then his jaw clamped shut beneath the roached mustache.

He stood like that and watched the pair ride away from him—his eyes glittering, his face warped in cruel and baffled fury.

11

Malloy was glad enough to be leaving Circle C behind, and also to have the spindly, worried-looking sheriff for a companion. He had deliberately manuevered this, knowing it would force Caslon to forget further ambush plans for the time being. The lawman was not bright, but still Caslon must know he had to be handled with a certain amount of tact.

As they rode at an easy gait, to the creak of saddle leather and rhythm of hoofs, Mark Malloy studied the man beside him and noted again the sheriff's dull-eyed tiredness. He asked, presently, "No luck hunting those road-gang outlaws?"

Legg gave him a sharp, frowning stare. "What do you know about that?"

"Only what I heard in town—that you were busy these days looking for them up in the hills. And I see you're coming in without 'em."

"Hoss threw a shoe," the sheriff grumbled. "I had to quit and come down in to Caslon's for a new one. Then, too, a man's just got to rest once in a while. Damned if I know where them crooks are holed up," he went on bitterly. "I've looked and looked!"

"Could be they're already long gone from here?" Malloy suggested.

"How? They got no horses. No guns, or grub, either." The sheriff shook his head. "Damned if it ain't got me beat!"

Mark Malloy discreetly let the subject drop.

They came, at length, to the fork in the road, where a branch led off toward his homestead. Here Malloy reined in.

"Well," he said, "I guess this is where I leave you. Pleased to have made your acquaintance, Sheriff."

Legg nodded, abstractedly. He had stopped when Malloy did; now, as the other man pulled aside into the branch trail, he touched spur and, without waiting for an invitation, calmly turned in behind him.

Wondering, Malloy glanced back. He could read absolutely nothing in that vacuous face, with its expression of constant, brooding puzzlement. They jogged along in silence for another twenty minutes, following the dim and winding wagon tracks in to the glen where the lonely cabin stood. As Malloy halted, Legg's horse came abreast of his own and stopped as though of its own accord.

They sat like that a moment.

"Well—" said Malloy, finally. He waited, but no flicker of intelligence crossed that other face. Entirely at a loss, and beginning to feel some annoyance, he shrugged and swung down.

Wordlessly he stripped his horse, turned the gelding loose. Legg hadn't moved during all this; but when Malloy stooped to gather up his heavy saddle and gear and carry them to the house, the sheriff hitched a long leg over and stepped down, directly at his heels. As Malloy halted to deposit his burden on a corner of the stoop beside the door, Legg opened the door and walked inside. Entering a moment later, the other found him seated comfortably in one of the chairs by the table, his hat on one knee.

"You shouldn't ought to do it," said Joe Legg, without warning.

The unexpectedness of it jarred a question out of the other. "Do what?"

"Rile Mr. Caslon that way. He's a hard man when he's riled, and he wants this piece of property awful bad. You ought to at least asked him what he'd pay you for it. Really, I think you should."

"Is that what you been chewing on, all the way here from Circle C?" Mark Malloy demanded, in considerable contempt. He kicked another chair away from the wall, straddled it with his arms folded across its back. "I'm a hard man myself, mister. And I don't mind saying that few things rile me more than being told what to do by a fool—a range-hog's fool of a bought-and-paid-for-sheriff, at that!"

If Joe Legg took offense, he didn't show it. He worked at something silently for a while. Finally, he said, "Mr. Malloy, I'm a man that does a lot of thinkin'. I guess you could say that I'm thinkin' about something or other, pretty near most of the time. . . ."

"I'd noticed that," Malloy put in, drily.

"A thinkin' man," Legg went on, "don't lose his temper as quick as ordinary people. Me, now, I could get awful mad at somebody that spoke to me like you just did; but, bein' thoughtful, I don't let myself. It ain't using your brain to put yourself in the way of crossing somebody that's probably a faster man with a gun!"

"You call that philosophy?" said Malloy, in a cold voice. "I call it playing the safe odds. I suppose whenever being a choreboy for Pitt Caslon gets in the way of behaving like an honest-to-God sheriff, you scrounge around till you find some way to justify it. That likely keeps you pretty busy, all right."

Legg shook his head, with an unhappy expression. "There you go, tryin' to make me mad!" he complained. "I'm no choreboy, as you call it. I'm a sheriff—a blamed good one! Two terms in office, so far, and I've yet to hear a complaint."

"Of course! If anybody opened his mouth about the way this county is run Caslon would let Tony Balter close it for him. Incidentally, have you ever tried giving Tony Balter any of your advice?"

"Well, now," said Legg, uncomfortably, "Tony, he ain't a man that does much thinkin'—"

"*That's* the truth!" Malloy grunted. "He's a trigger-crazy killer—who can get away with anything because Pitt Caslon stands behind him. He and two other Circle C men tried to run me to earth this morning and murder me; which is the truth, too, and you know it!

"But what good would it do me if I tried to bring any of

them to court? Would you so much as serve a warrant?"

The sheriff couldn't answer that question. He squirmed painfully, and ran one bony hand across his fierce black mustache. "We ain't getting nowhere," he complained, finally. "I wanted to talk things over with you but you keep changing the subject. About this property, now—"

"All right, what about it!" snapped Malloy. "You'd like me to sell out to Pitt Caslon, at this terms, and not make trouble. Is that the best advice your deep thinking has been able to cook up for me?"

"What need have you got for a spread like this one?" the sheriff insisted. "You're a townsman, Malloy. You come here where you don't belong, mix into things you don't half understand! You'll end up just making trouble for everybody, yourself concerned—when, if you'll only use your head and take the deal Pitt Caslon says he's ready to make . . ."

"And what about the Garretts? And all the other ranchers, big and small, that Caslon is determined to drive off of Hermit Flats?" Mark Malloy shook his head. "No, mister! Just one thing you've had to say was true: I never knew the size of the thing I was bidding into, until I got into it. But now I do know, and I think I'll play the hand that was dealt me. As for causing trouble—why, that's up to Caslon. I'll cause as much as he asks for!"

There was a moment's heavy silence. "Sounds like your mind's made up, don't it?" Joe Legg said, finally, and with a sigh he unfolded his beanpole length and picked his sweat-marked hat off the table. "I was afraid you'd be like this, from what I'd heard about you; now I'm right fearful of what will happen as a result. I'm warning you, though: You better hew close to the line, Malloy! I'll not take much off a foreigner that comes into my bailiwick and stirs things up!"

Malloy didn't bother to answer. He too had risen, pushing aside the chair he had straddled. He stood by to let the sheriff precede him through the doorway and out into the warm glare of the sun. And at the very edge of the stoop, saw Joe Legg halt with his anxious frowning look set on something at his feet.

Imprinted in the soft earth was the plain mark of a footprint—a shapeless, massive prison shoe. Malloy caught his breath, waiting for the sheriff's startled questions—all too conscious of the damage that could be worked against him, just now, with a charge of harboring escaped criminals.

But next moment Joe Legg had stepped down off the porch and he went over to his waiting horse, that same puzzled scowl imprinted on his features. Very slowly, it dawned on Mark Malloy that Legg hadn't even seen the footprint. The constant and ponderous churning of the sheriff's mind, working at its endless problems, must blind him much of the time to things that lay directly before his eyes. Small wonder then that he'd had no luck finding sign of the chain-gang fugitives, up in the hills. . . .

After he had watched the sheriff out of sight and had heard the last echoes of his horse's hoofs die among the timber, Mark Malloy took a long breath and turned to face the choice he had made—or which had, rather, been forced upon him. It was not even yet too late, he supposed. He could gain nothing by trying to hold this ground against all the power of Circle C.

Why not take Caslon's purchase offer? Why not pack his saddlebags, mount up, and ride away from here, letting the Garretts and Circle C fight their war out between them?

He knew he would not, for with all his faults, he was no Joe Legg—taking the easy course, while all the time searching out excuses to assuage his outraged moral feelings. But that wasn't entirely it, either. More than a little of his stubborn determination was born of a wish—one that was unworthy, perhaps, of such a cold-headed realist as he prided himself on being: a wish that Jean Garrett should be forced to admit her error in labeling him a tool of Pitt Caslon's.

If I've made a mistake, she had said, *I suppose some day I'll have to apologize.* And some day, he intended she should do just that. . . .

When he entered the cabin again, therefore, it was not to pack his saddlebags but, instead, to take from them a work shirt and a pair of jeans. With a sigh he stripped out of his expensive town clothing and hung these up, paying careful attention to the crease of the trousers.

Scowling into the shaving mirror, he told his reflection: "Well, you make one devil of a homesteader—but now you at least come a little nearer to looking the part!" Afterwards, reminded by the sun and by his revived appetite that it was crowding dinnertime, he stirred up a meal from the dwindling supplies in the storeroom.

An inventory, he decided, was first in order, to discover exactly what he had on hand and what he would be needing. The list he drew up consisted mostly of foodstuffs—and in sizeable quantities, against the possible necessity of standing off a lone-handed siege. He must not forget a box or two of shells for the .38; and perhaps, for greater firepower at longer range, a rifle.

Malloy had never owned a saddle gun, but he had shot at still targets a few times and knew how to handle one. With plenty of ammunition for practice purposes, and time to spend on it, he thought he could quickly develop sufficient skill with the weapon.

Toward evening, a tattered roof of clouds slid over the hills and rain fell—not any great amount, or with any fury, but enough to give a certain assurance that Circle C wouldn't be in saddle that night, to offer him trouble. Caslon must still feel that the tinhorn at Indian Springs was someone to be disposed of at his convenience; he wouldn't see any need of a wet ride by night, when he could pick his own time for the job.

So Mark Malloy settled comfortably in a chair pulled over by the open door, and smoked down one of his thin cheroots as he listened to the friendly voices of the storm, and watched the birches by the spring leap and darken in an occasional flicker of lightning while thunder rumbled off among the hills.

The cabin roof was not exactly tight, after all, he discovered, and for a few minutes he was kept busy setting out pots and pans to catch the separate drippings. The oddly musical sounds they made added to the pleasant murmur of the rain;

tomorrow, he planned to tackle the roof and patch the holes with more flattened tins, though he would probably flatten his thumb also in the process. He smiled a little, thinly, as he thought of the unfamiliar skills he would most likely be acquiring if he stayed here long.

The storm played out. Before retiring, he took his .38 and made a circuit of the cabin through dark and dripping trees, alert for any possible sign of danger. He detected none; nor did anything occur that might disturb his uneasy slumber.

It was toward midmorning that his bay gelding brought him once more into the little cow-country village of Hermit Flats. The clouds had gone, as though they never were; a high sun was steaming the moisture of the thirsty ground. Rain had no more than settled the dust, and within hours the dust devils would be walking again across these Flats, before the swirling push of the parched and heated wind.

Town did not much resemble the excited scene when he last rode away from here, after his meeting with Tony Balter. A few horses were racked at tie-poles along the main street but a quick survey found only brands from the smaller ranches whose herds ranged the lower Flats. Malloy kept an alert watch for Circle C riders, though, as he dismounted and tied near a water trough just outside the mercantile whose upper rooms housed Frank Downing's law office.

When he turned away, with a jerk to test the knot in his horse's reins, he was a little surprised to find Downing himself leaning his loose-hung frame against the building corner, where there had been no one a moment before. Thumbs thrust into waistband, narrow-brimmed hat set at the back of his head of crisply curling hair, the lawyer gave him a short nod; and his sardonic mouth was twisted in evident amusement.

"Well, well!" murmured Downing. "I saw you ride in, but at first I couldn't really be sure it was you, in that get-up. You look quite bucolic."

Malloy saw no reason to answer and merely waited, his

regard unfriendly. The lawyer, undismayed by lack of encouragement, blandly continued.

"And you're still alive! That's reason for congratulations!" He hitched himself erect, with a jerk of his head toward the office stairs. "Step up with me and have a drink on it."

"In that rat's nest?" Malloy shook his head. "No, thanks," he said, flatly. "Mainly because I never drink, this time of day; but also, because that place of yours depresses me!"

For an instant, then, a current of real animosity flowed between these two who were, in a way, somehow much alike. They were about of a height, Downing perhaps an inch or two the taller. They had in common, moreover, a sort of suavity and confidence of bearing that in the lawyer was fined to a brittle edge of mocking cynicism. But for now the masks were down, and each took the other's measure. And it was Downing who broke the brief silence, with that characteristic lift of shoulders as though pulling his gaunt, loose-framed shape together.

"You don't give much of a damn, do you," he said, thinly, "whether you've got anybody on your side or not? You might wish, before this thing is over, that you had me!"

"No," said Malloy. "Because you're never on anybody's side, Frank—except your own! From the first, you've been giving me a play; yet all the time you were only measuring me, trying to fit me somewhere into your own pet schemes. Well, I'm telling you, as of now, to quit it! Just leave me clear out of your calculations—because I won't play."

Downing's eyes narrowed; his mouth grew bitter. "You cheap tinhorn!" he muttered, his whole manner gone quickly hard and ugly. "Go ahead, damn you—crowd your luck, and your nerve! We'll see who's around when the final cards are down." But then, overcoming this brief break of anger, the man got back his control and his mouth twisted again with that easy, mocking smile.

"I have an idea," he said, "that Pitt Caslon has a little surprise up his sleeve for you. It must be something important that would bring him dusting into town an hour ago, to hole up with that stupid sheriff in the court house. He's in there now. I don't know what's on the fire, but you may be finding out—sooner than you like."

"Thanks," said Malloy drily. "Thanks for nothing."

Turning away, he shouldered through the door into the mercantile. He felt Downing's cool stare following him.

12

THE DARK INTERIOR was redolent with the familiar smells of a country store—of leather, and cloth goods, of sorghum and tobacco and coal oil. The place was empty, but after a moment the storekeeper came padding out of his cubbyhole office at the rear. When he saw who his customer was, and saw the length of the list Malloy had fetched from his pocket, he showed a high excitement.

"Then it's true?" he blurted. "You're really moving in at the Springs?"

Malloy regarded him coldly. "Any reason why not?" he challenged. "It strikes me as a nice, quiet place for a man to settle down a spell—and mind his own business!"

The man colored at this barbed comment, and turned away without further comment to start filling the order. Malloy watched him work, frowning over the fact that he and his doings should be a topic of such keen and general gossip. He inspected briefly the foodstuffs and supplies that were set out for him on the store counter. The proprietor handed him back his list finally, pointing at two of the items.

"I can't give you the Winchester, or the shells," he said. "You'll have to try the gunsmith over on C Street."

Malloy folded up the list, pocketing it. "I figured to. What's the tab on this stuff?" When it had been added and he had checked the man's arithmetic, he settled his bill and said, "I'll hire a rig at the livery, and be back."

A familiar voice said, dubiously, "You may, or you may not."

Looking around quickly, Malloy saw the sheriff frowning at him. He hadn't heard Joe Legg enter and, remembering

what Downing had told him earlier, knew a stirring of alarm.
"What's up? You want me for something?"

"A little talk," Joe Legg told him. "A matter that's come
up. . . . You mind stepping down to my office with me?"

"Could be that I do mind—if you're running errands for
Pitt Caslon again!"

"This is official business," Legg insisted. "You better come.
I wouldn't want to have to get tough."

"*You?*" grunted Malloy. But he turned with a shrug to tell
the storekeeper: "Hold my order, will you? I'll be back."

He fell in beside the lawman. They met no one, passing
along the empty street to the court house, and yet Malloy
had little doubt that town gossip was chronicling their every
step. The storekeeper could be depended upon for that.

On his own part, Malloy thought it entirely too clear that
something unpleasant was waiting for him at the sheriff's
office—a surprise, perhaps, that Pitt Caslon had prepared
for him. He was all the more certain of this when, preceding
Legg down the dark and musty hallway, he first glimpsed
the Circle C boss through the office doorway and saw the
look on Caslon's smugly pleased and expectant face.

He didn't like that look, at all. Crossing the threshold, he
quickly heeled around into a position where he could face
the room and the doorway as well. Joe Legg had halted there,
himself watching Pitt Caslon and plainly waiting for him to
start the proceedings; but Caslon, leaning back comfortably
with his chair tilted against the wall, seemed in no hurry.

There was a fourth person in the room, who leaned against
the edge of the sheriff's desk yonder, underneath the bulletin
board where wanted notices were posted. Malloy looked at
him with a slow, inquiring glance, saw in him a nondescript
type of cowhand—trail-dirty, now, and with a three-day
growth of beard clouding his jowls. There was a certain
vicious quality about his brash stare, however, that made
Malloy wonder more than a little if he didn't carry the
brand of killer.

He looked at Pitt Caslon again. "All right," he said. "Stop

licking your chops and let's get ahead with this. What have you cooked up this time?"

Slowly, a grin spread across Caslon's broad face, narrowing his greenish eyes. "I'm not real sure yet," he answered. "But from what Steve Wendell tells me, I got an idea it might turn out to be a charge of murder!"

"Oh?" Malloy favored Wendell with a cold and unrevealing stare, and waited.

"Ed Renke's murder," Caslon finished.

"I just come back through Saunderstown," the man by the desk put in, harshly. "I learned there about Renke being killed in an alley, under peculiar-lookin' circumstances. And now, you show up with Renke's homestead patent."

Mark Malloy's disciplined exterior gave, he was sure, no hint of emotion whatsoever. To the sheriff he said, "You read that to mean that I killed him?"

Legg made a gesture. "Well . . ."

"How else can it be read?" snapped Caslon.

"One other way," Malloy said, and put his stare directly on the Circle C boss. "It goes something like this:

"After Ed Renke absconded with that homestead patent, a couple of gunhands were sent to find him and fetch it back. They trailed Renke as far as Saunderstown, and there they trapped him in a dark alley behind a saloon and finished him off—only, in doing it, the one who did the murder was killed, himself. This I know for sure; because—I killed him!

"The second one," Malloy went on, levelly, "was Steve Wendell, here; I've been wondering all along what became of him afterwards. I suppose he hung around town for several days, trying to find out what had happened to the patent. Finally he must have learned that I'd won it off of Renke just before the shooting. So he followed me here and reported to his boss—to the man who had ordered Renke's murder. To you, Caslon!"

Steve Wendell had come up off the edge of the desk, his face gone thunderous; even Pitt Caslon's confidence had lost a little of its smug certainty, had taken on an edge of danger.

"Sheriff!" he cried, suddenly. "We're wasting time! Book this man, and then take him downstairs and lock him up!"

The sharp command had its effect on Joe Legg, prodding the lawman so that he took an uncertain step toward Malloy. The latter said, "Better stay where you are!" and this quiet-spoken warning checked the sheriff. Legg merely stood un-moving, and watched Malloy start a hand toward the gap of his brush jacket.

"Get 'em up, Malloy!"

Head whipping around, he saw the danger—too late; Steve Wendell, with a smooth swiftness that branded him plainly for the gunman Malloy had already figured him, had palmed a sixshooter and he stood crouched a little, the point of the weapon covering the gambler. "Don't touch that hideout, mister!" he snapped. "It's quick suicide!"

Chagrin was a bitter taste in his mouth as Malloy slowly withdrew his hand, empty. He told Wendell, icily, "You're piling up a score, fast! They can't hold me on this phony charge—and when the time comes that I get out of here, you and I have a settlement coming."

For answer the gunman merely snickered, emboldened by the advantage a drawn sixshooter gave him. Pitt Caslon cut off any further talk. "Lock him up, Sheriff!" he repeated, curtly. "Take that stingy gun away from him and put him where he can't make trouble. Better keep him covered, Steve, or he might prove tricky."

Joe Legg moved forward now, his face a little drained of color and his scowl more worried than ever. While Malloy stood motionless he reached in under the jacket, fumbled the gun from his clip holster, and laid it on the desk.

The sheriff had a weapon out of its scarred holster by this time, but Steve Wendell seemed in no hurry to put his own away. "I'll just go along," he said, "to make sure you get him locked up safe. . . ."

It was briefly done. Malloy kept his jaw tight-shut, after the first angry protest, for he knew arguments would get him nothing. He let himself be herded, at gunpoint, down the long and musty corridor, through a heavy door and down a few steps into the clammy cell-block that made up the court-house basement. It smelled badly here, of mice and unwashed bodies and stale mop-water; Malloy's fastidious senses were revolted and it took a prodding gunbarrel to make him descend into that noisome darkness.

None of the three tiny cells was occupied. Malloy was shoved into one of them and as the door closed on him he tried a last appeal with the sheriff. "I hope you realize there's such a thing as suing for false arrest," he said. "And that the longer you hold me here, the more trouble I can make for you later on. I didn't kill Ed Renke and I can prove it!"

Joe Legg was plainly troubled all right; if they had been alone, he might have made some headway with him. But Wendell was there to break the talking up, and to remind the sheriff that he was obeying Pitt Caslon's orders. "You'll stay here," the gunman told Malloy, "until you're set loose. So you might as well make yourself comfortable. . . ."

That last held a malicious sarcasm. Alone, Malloy glanced about him with a shudder at the dirty, foul and airless cub-byhole where he had been stored for safekeeping. An iron shelf fastened against the wall by a couple of chains, and without any kind of bedding, was the only comfort afforded him. The barred window that gave him light was very high and very small, set flush with the level of the ground.

Whatever Caslon's purpose in jailing him, on a charge which he must know could not be made to stick, the Circle C boss had certainly won this particular round. How much, though, could it gain him?

Time!

Yes, he knew with quick insight; that must be it. Something was afoot—and waiting here in this foul-smelling lock-up beneath the court house, he could only wonder helplessly just what scheme Pitt Caslon was even now involved in carrying out.

An hour, and more, dragged out. Few sounds reached him in his prison, except the creaking of timbers in the old build-ing overhead, and the street noises through the high window. Then the door at the head of the stairs swung open and the sheriff came down into the cell room, looking more worried than ever. He said, gruffly, "A visitor, Malloy. I'll leave you alone with him," he told the newcomer, "but I don't think I dast let you into the cell. You can stand outside and talk to him. Five minutes."

Malloy, seated on the iron bunk, looked up with interest as his caller appeared in the shadowy corridor beyond the door. He had no idea whom he expected to see there; he was surprised and not particularly pleased to find that it was Frank Downing.

"You?" he grunted, not rising.

Downing leaned a shoulder against the bars of the door, peered in at him with something close to amusement quirking his cynical face. "Apparently. I don't know, really, why I bother—especially after some of the remarks you made to me this morning. But after all, I'm a lawyer; and I'd say that right now you were a man who could use one.

"So I told our fine, deep-thinking sheriff that I had been retained, and reminded him of the law which says every prisoner has the right of counsel. Pitt Caslon not being around to tell him what to do, I was able to scare him into letting me down here."

"Caslon's left town?"

"Some time ago—headed back to Circle C, I think. He was looking pleased and full of purpose."

Malloy scowled, not liking this information. "And exactly why are you getting into the thing?" he demanded, shrewdly.

"For purely selfish reasons—though they happen to coincide with yours. You could rot in this jail, Malloy, for all I care; but I don't like to see Caslon win such an easy victory. So I'd say we should get to work and see how we're going to pry you loose."

"If you're serious about it," Malloy said, "I guess I can't be particular. Because I'm certainly not going to sit here until Pitt Caslon's ready to turn me out. . . . Where's the closest telegraph key?"

"At the railroad—Mustang Station. But it's anyway a five-hour ride."

"Go there, and send a wire off to the town marshal at Saunderstown—ask him for the full details of the killing of Ed Renke. If you can, get statements from two witnesses: Bob Osgood, and Chris Henning. With those in hand, nobody can hold me here."

Downing, all business now, had paper and pencil to jot down the names Malloy had given him. Pocketing them, he nodded, crisply. "All right, we'll see. Meanwhile—" He smiled with a secret, malicious pleasure. "I'll try not to grieve too much, as I think of you cooling your heels in these pleasant surroundings. Enjoy yourself, friend. And be sure you don't leave before I get back."

Mark Malloy snarled at him. "Quit wasting time. If there's a five-hour ride ahead of you, you better find yourself a horse and get started."

"In good time—in good time. Don't loose patience!" The lawyer's jeering chuckle trailed after him as he turned, unhurriedly, and sauntered back to the stairway.

Now, time indeed stood still for the prisoner in the cell. It in no way helped to realize that only selfish interest would stir the lawyer to prod himself at all. Five hours at least to Mustang Station and five hours back, with the further time needed for a wire to be sent and answered; add to this the possibility that, even when confronted with the true facts of the killing, Pitt Caslon's sheriff might not be persuaded to act on them, and turn his prisoner loose. . . . These were the bleak thoughts that worried him, as he sat on the hard cot or toured the meager dimensions of the ill-smelling, airless jail cell.

Dusk came, and with it came the sheriff to start a lamp burning dimly somewhere at the far end of the lockup, and bring him a plate of food that looked none too palatable. He refused to talk, leaving Malloy alone once more to face the prospect of a night spent trying to find rest on the hard iron bunk.

However, in spite of his sour conviction that sleep was an impossibility, it did creep up on him and took him nearly by surprise. The dim seepage of gray dawn through the murky darkness found him stretched out on the unyielding bunk, rousing with sharp pains in cramped muscles and a dull headache.

He could have wished longer for the oblivion of sleep, because waking meant only the start of another siege of restless waiting. And in fact this second day was well along when, in dull disbelief, Malloy finally heard the clang of the big door opening, and the voices of Frank Downing and the sheriff approaching his cell.

There was no argument; apparently the lawyer, and the telegram he had brought back with him, had already settled Joe Legg's troubled mind. In complete submission the sheriff opened Malloy's cell, and without comment handed over the .38 from the drawer in the office desk. But it was plain from his look that he had never done harder thinking in his whole career than he was doing at this moment.

Frank Downing told him, "You've finally got your tail in a crack and you aren't going to be able to pull it loose. It was bound to come to this—the law crowding you from one side, and Pitt Caslon from the other. I'm just as pleased not to be in your boots!"

He got no answer, and a moment later the two emerged from the gloomy court-house building; the touch of clean sunlight was good after the dank chill of the cell. Malloy felt dirty, saturated with foul, damp rot. He would have welcomed a shave and a bath, just then, and a change of clothing from the hideout. But these luxuries must wait a little longer.

Downing, haggard and unkempt himself, said heavily, "Well, it's up to you now! I did my part, and I'm beat out— that's the longest stretch of saddle work I've done in five years. I'm going to bed! But you better be hitting the road."

"I suppose you're right." Malloy looked at the other man. "I won't bother to thank you for getting me out—I know it was for your own interests or you wouldn't have bothered. We understand each other pretty well, Downing."

"As long as we do," the lawyer answered, "we should manage to get along."

Malloy favored him with a slow, speculative regard. "Maybe," he said. "I wouldn't be too sure of it—you may end up sadly disappointed. This once we were on the same side of the fence; another time we might line up differently."

Contempt rimmed the other's voice as he answered. "I said before—no cheap tinhorn can put a scare into me. Don't try it!"

"We'll see," murmured Malloy, quietly. "Some of these days, we almost certainly will see. . . ."

13

HE WENT DIRECTLY to the gunsmith's shop on C Street, resuming his chores just where they had been interrupted twenty-four hours ago. There he bought a Winchester repeater which the old man told him had been newly rebuilt and for whose accuracy and easy action he would personally vouch; having checked the throw of the bolt and the trigger-pull a few times, Malloy paid cash for the weapon, and for the shells he needed. Some impulse prompted him to break open a box of rifle shells and load the chamber, before he stepped out on the street carrying the Winchester over one arm.

At the livery, he got his saddle horse and also hired a light rig and team; and with the bay mare tied at the tailgate of the wagon he rode around to the mercantile. Apparently the news of his release from jail had been a little slow in getting spread about; the storekeeper greeted him with an expression of astonishment, and Malloy told the man, irritably, "Well, I said I'd be back for those things I bought. What do you say we get them rustled outside, and into the wagon?"

The man started stammering. "Sure—sure, Mr. Malloy. No time at all!" But it soon proved that he had scattered the order and returned it to the shelves, apparently certain that Malloy would not be back to claim his purchases. With considerable incoherent stammering, he hastily set to work reassembling the cans and bags and boxes, and dumping them into the wagon tied before the store.

When the work had been finished, and the tailgate fastened, Malloy dismissed the man with a shrug and climbed to his place on the hard wooden seat. He was no expert with the lines, but these were a lazy pair of horses that needed a touch of the rein-ends to keep them moving at all. Feeling conspicuous on the high seat, he got his team to moving and went rolling through the dust of the town's streets.

He was not to leave entirely without incident, however. He had almost reached the big court house when a shout lifted him to attention; across the way, a figure had appeared at a saloon entrance. Even as he looked, the batwing doors winnowed and a second man appeared beside the first. This one, he saw, was Steve Wendell—and both were starting forward into the street.

Malloy might have tried whipping his horses into a run, to take him away from there. Instead, he groped for and located the smooth metal of the new bought rifle beneath his feet; he brought it up, flipped the ejector, slanting blued barrel across his body with its muzzle covering the approaching men.

"Keep back!" he ordered. His voice ran sharply across the stillness.

But Wendell had already started reaching for the six-shooter that jutted from his holster, and without any compunction Malloy worked the trigger. A rifle was not really a familiar weapon to him, however; he shot wide, the bullet kicking up road dust inches to the side of his target.

Sunlight winked on metal then as Steve Wendell cleared his sixgun, and before Malloy had time to kick out the empty cartridge the Circle C man fired. But Wendell failed to take advantage of this fraction of time; he hurried too much, at the last instant, and his bullet was a wild miss. And then, taking better aim, Malloy squeezed off a second shot.

It knocked his opponent down. Wendell threw his gun away and went rolling in the dust, and a high scream tore from him to mingle with the echoes of the shooting.

The team, frightened, had started pitching and bucking against the brake shoe. Quickly Malloy went over the wheel into the deep ruts, where he could have solid footing. Levering a new shell into the breech, he looked about for the other man who had been with Wendell; but that one had disappeared. A flurry of hoofbeats, fading out, told what had become of him, however. At sight of Wendell's defeat he had turned back and beat a hasty retreat to the horse he must have had waiting for him, around at the side of the saloon building.

Trailing the rifle, Malloy walked over to Steve Wendell. The man lay where he had fallen, writhing in the dust that was turning red with his blood. Peal after peal of agonized screaming broke from his distorted mouth. It took only a glance to see that his right arm had been smashed by the heavy rifle slug.

Malloy looked at him, oddly without emotion. He was, in a way, glad not to have killed again—even though this man had given him plenty of provocation. With his gunarm ruined, Wendell would never again be sent out to hunt down a man and herd him into a murder trap, as he had done to Ed Renke in Saunderstown. Nor would he be likely to take any part henceforth in the dangerous business of hanging a lying frameup on an innocent man.

"You better stop that yelling," Malloy said, "and get on your feet and find yourself a doctor." But his words fell on ears deafened by agony, and with a shrug he turned away, his attention caught by a movement a few yards from him.

There, on the steps of the court house, Joe Legg stood watching. Slowly, Mark Malloy walked over to face the sheriff. "All right!" he challenged. "What will it be, mister? Two of them jumped me, and I shot in self-defense. But Pitt Caslon will probably pin a medal on you if you jail me for attempted murder. You want to try and do him that little favor, Legg?"

They looked at each other during long moments, Malloy waiting for a move and only able to guess at the thoughts working behind the sheriff's troubled scowl. Then, however, he saw a change; he saw Joe Legg's stooped shoulders take on an even greater sagging, saw a beaten tiredness come into the rail-thin frame of the man.

With heavy slowness, Joe Legg turned about. He opened the door of the court house, and he shuffled through and pulled the door shut behind him. . . . And Mark Malloy knew he had just witnessed the ordeal of a man who had engaged in his last, inward debate with a tortured conscience—and lost.

Yonder, Steve Wendell had already pulled himself to his feet and gone staggering away through the dust, shattered arm dripping blood. From a dozen doors and windows, shadowed eyes were watching, but otherwise the town seemed lost as before in the quiet somnolence of a late summer afternoon.

Returning to his wagon, Malloy climbed again to the seat and got it rolling—on his way toward whatever might be waiting for him at the homestead at Indian Springs.

He was nearly in sight of the place—separated from it, in fact, only by a shoulder of rock around which the trail looped just ahead—when an alien sound gave him the first hint of an answer to his question.

That sound was the lowing of a steer.

Malloy's head jerked at the noise; his spine, weary of the jogging wagon seat, stiffened quickly. He was sure there had been no cattle within four miles of his homestead yesterday morning; and while it was possible that a few head might have strayed this far to water he had an instant conviction that such was not the case. Flashing the lines, he lifted dust off the rumps of his team as he sent the rig rolling forward, to clear that jumble of granite outcrop and buck brush and give him a view of the sloping acres of his land.

His guess had been right. Circle C beef had been moved onto the Indian Springs homestead; at least a hundred head of them. They grazed the sparse bunch grass of the upward slopes, waded knee-deep in the rushes and the swampy level about the spring. Yonder, three saddle horses, all bearing Caslon's iron, were tied near the cabin; and a twist of piñon smoke lifted into late golden sunlight from the stovepipe chimney. Pitt Caslon had moved in on him.

It took only a moment to digest this, and it took no longer for the gun in Malloy's holster to slip into his hand. But the

sound of a revolver hammer earing back to full cock halted
him before he could make any other move. A voice at Malloy's back ordered, harshly, "Just drop the stingy gun, mister, and hoist 'em. And be careful doin' it!"

He cursed himself, bitterly; even though forewarned, he
had let himself be tolled neatly into a trap. Malloy opened
his hand and let the .38 fall from it, to plop into the dirt
beside the wagon's high front wheel.

Not looking around, he heard boots scrape as a man
jumped down from the top of the rock, strode forward with
spike heels crunching. He came into sight, sixshooter at the
ready, and stooped briefly to pick up Malloy's handgun. The
man was Dick Ford, the Caslon rider.

"I been watchin' for you," Ford said, grinning. "We got
word you was loose and on your way." He shoved the captured revolver into the pocket of his coat, after a contemptuous glance at the size of the weapon. "Where's the rifle
you used on Steve Wendell?" he added.

He found this, leaning against the dashboard. Snatching
it down, he holstered his sixshooter and swung the muzzle of
Malloy's own Winchester to threaten the prisoner. "All
right!" he grunted. "You're defanged. Now, slide over, and
take this rig where I tell you to."

In black despair Malloy made room for him on the seat;
and when Ford had swung up, with a single easy motion,
they went rolling like that toward the cabin.

The door opened, and a man came out and watched with an
arm lifted to shield his eyes from the stab of the westering
sun. This one said, "Got him?"

"Got him," answered Ford. "And a rigful of vittles; so at
least we won't get hungry, batching it in this damned shack.
Real considerate, I figure."

"Yeah," said the man in the doorway. He turned, and
yelled into the cabin, behind him. "Tony!"

Dick Ford punched Malloy with the rifle. "Climb down,
brother! There's a man here that's been wanting to see you!"

Whatever happened now, he knew it was going to be bad.
It was with the greatest reluctance that he wrapped his lines

around the brake handle, stepped to the hub of the front wheel and from there dropped to the ground. He was just turning as Tony Balter strode through the cabin doorway.

"Here he is, Tony," said Dick Ford.

No one else spoke. There was no movement, either, for a long moment while Tony Balter stood with thick legs spread, head thrust forward, crazy eyes staring at the man he hated. His head was bare, and the weak light of the dying sun lay unshadowed across the face of the man, pointing up the glitter of his mean eyes, the working of his taut, tense mouth.

"At last!" he whispered, in triumphant gloating. "At last, damn you. . . ."

Balter's arms began to lift, slowly, his splayed hands drawing up and back, inching nearer to the twin gunbutts that bracketed his slabby hips. The fingers, stubby and strong and each backed by its mat of black fur, twitched slightly with the intensity of the man's emotion. And now Balter started moving forward, step by slow step, his burning gaze never wavering from the face of Mark Malloy.

Malloy took his hand from the rim of the wagon wheel and turned carefully to meet the other, a dead hopelessness riding every limb and lying like lead within his belly. The waiting silence seemed like a brittle thing that could crack in two with the weight of a word. And Dick Ford said that word, blurting it suddenly, his face gone white with sick horror: "He ain't got a gun, Tony!"

His outburst stopped the killer, seemed to haul him up the way a check rein stops a horse in its tracks. Like a man coming out of a trance, he straightened slowly, some of the tautness going from him. His hands dropped away from the holstered weapons.

Then, as Malloy's breathing began to function again at the realization that death had passed him, though by the narrowest of margins, the right arm of Tony Balter came arcing suddenly forward and a fist smashed solidly against the gambler's face, stunning him with surprise and pain and driving him backward.

His shoulders struck the wagon box, and this saved him

from going down. But before he could get his footing that fist drove into him again, with all the killer's frenzy behind it. Malloy went clear around, this time, and rammed head on into the side of the wagon. His hands groped for a hold on something to support him; his knees buckled and he slewed down into the dirt.

Through the buzzing of pain his numbed hearing caught Tony Balter's panted words: "Tote him inside. Then get busy unloading this wagon, and run the horses into the corral. Caslon has business to finish with this skunk. After he's got his hands on that homestead patent, then I'll have my turn. I can wait... . ."

Malloy was trying to get hands and knees under him when he was grabbed under the arms and unceremoniously hauled the short distance to the cabin, his heels trailing. "On the bunk," Dick Ford grunted. "He'll be out of the way there." Boots thudded over floorboards. Then the Circle C men had dumped their prisoner onto the musty blankets, and left him there.

He lay like that, head still spinning from the crushing blows of Balter's fist. And in him was the cruel knowledge that a moment's carelessness had lost this high-card gamble for him—and, with it, the hope of life itself.

14

H E FELT STRONG enough, presently, to push up to a sitting position on the edge of the bunk, clinging to the wooden frame while the room settled itself. Looking around, he saw that the cabin was filled with a warm golden glow, dust motes swimming in the shaft of sunset light coming through the window. Over at the stove, the Circle C rider whose name he didn't know was stirring up some food. Through the open door, Malloy saw Tony Balter and Dick Ford standing on the narrow stoop, talking.

When the prisoner came up off the bunk, the cook dropped his skillet and made a move toward his holstered gun; but Malloy shook his head. "Don't get jumpy," he muttered. "I have to have some fresh air. I don't feel so good." Not waiting for argument, he went across the room on unsteady legs, eased through the open door.

The pair outside turned sharply but he ignored them; he went to the edge of the stoop and sat down there, arms on his knees, head hanging limply as he looked at the ground between his boots and felt the cool breath of evening begin to stir across his bloody face.

Above him, Tony Balter made a savage, scornful remark: "Enjoy the sunset, tinhorn. It's likely the last you'll ever see!"

Malloy made no answer, nor did he look at his enemies. He stayed as he was, and gradually the warmth began to die from the air about him. Raising his head, he saw that the shadows of the hills were creeping now into this hollow. Yonder, the topmost branches of the silver birches that lined the spring were shaking their leaves in the last of the sunlight, but within a few moments they too would lose their golden brightness and subside into dusky shadow.

"About time Caslon was getting here, ain't it?" Dick Ford wanted to know. His voice sounded odd in the silence that was broken only by the murmur of the spring. Tony Balter didn't bother to answer him.

A moment passed. Then, without warning, Mark Malloy pursed his lips and sent a few whistled notes to go floating into the stillness.

"What the hell do you think you're doing?" Tony Balter demanded, whirling on him.

"There's a whippoorwill has its nest on the slope yonder, in the brush," said Malloy, simply. "He starts up about this time of day, and I like to whistle back to him. You can't begrudge me a little pleasure like that, can you—it being the last evening of my life?"

Balter studied him through those narrow, hating eyes. Then, with a grunt of disdain, he turned away. Dick Ford, who had been listening, said, "I don't hear no damn whippoorwill."

"It's hard to fool him," said Malloy. "I only manage once in a while myself. I doubt if you could do it, at all."

"Who says I couldn't?" the Circle C rider demanded, bridling.

"Try it."

And he did, listening with head cocked for a long moment after the shrill notes died. No answering call came down from the brushy slope, where night was already gathering in the shadows under the scrub oaks. Tony Balter gave a derisive snort. "Ain't you something, though?"

Dick Ford began to get red; the color started in his flat cheeks and spread through his dark skin, but he kept a leash on his anger—it was too dangerous, losing one's temper with Tony Balter. All he permitted himself was to say, tightly, "Maybe you could do better?"

The cook came into the doorway. "What are you guys up to, anyhow?"

"Keep quiet!" snapped Tony Balter, and forthwith he

made his version of a whippoorwill's cry. It was a very good one, too; sitting there, Mark Malloy listened for an answer and began to know a deep despair that this last, feeble hope would prove a vain one. Then—

"There you are!" Balter's crow of satisfaction was entirely out of proportion to the size of his accomplishment. "Heard him that time, didn't you? Now, you satisfied?" He didn't wait for Dick Ford's reply; turning to the other Circle C man he said, harshly, "That grub ready yet? I'm starving!"

"It's gettin' cold waitin' for you. Come on in."

At an order from Balter, Malloy got to his feet and preceded the others into the shack. The lamp was burning, now, pushing back the encroaching shadows. Malloy returned to his seat on the bunk and the cook shoved a tin plate of beans and bacon into his hands, saying, "You might as well eat while you're setting. It's your own grub, after all."

Malloy took it with a nod of thanks; but he was far from hungry, thought of food revolting to nerves that were tight with the tension that had been building in him over the period of an hour. Outside in the dusk the whippoorwill cry sounded again, lonesomely, a couple of times, each seemingly a little nearer to the cabin, and then it fell off to silence as it got no answer.

Only the small change of conversation was passed about as the men ate, Ford and Balter seated at the trestle table, the other Circle C hand leaning shoulders against the rough wall. There was nothing wrong with Dick Ford's appetite; within seconds he had gulped down his mess of beans and black strap and his tin spoon was scraping the bottom of the plate. "Got any more of this slop?" he demanded.

"Get your own," growled the cook, pointing with his spoon at the skillet. "And shut up about the grub. Tomorrow it'll be your turn to cook, remember!"

The other shrugged and hitched back his chair, spoon rattling in the plate as he got up to move across toward the stove. The noise he was making must have covered any sound from the doorway; the first warning anyone had was the voice that spoke with startling abruptness: "All right, everybody stay just the way they are!" Heads lifted, then, and they were staring at the grotesque figure of big Ike, filling the doorway, his sixgun covering the room.

Dick Ford and the cook had been caught flatfooted and neither made any move to resist. But there was a clatter of tinware as Tony Balter dropped his knife and started a stabbing movement toward thonged holsters. From the window behind him a second voice rapped, "Don't do it!" It checked his move; and held that way, taut and dangerous as a cocked gun, he turned his bullet head slowly and his hot stare took in the face of Spud, just visible beyond the open window, his forearms resting on the sill and a second sixgun trained on Balter's blocky shape.

That was more than even Tony Balter would pit himself against. He raised his hands slowly and as though with a great effort; they were still crooked and formed to fit the gunhandles as he put them on the edge of the table in front of him.

"Fine!" said big Ike, when it was plain that no one was going to risk a break. "Maybe you'd better lift their guns, Malloy, just so they won't be tempted."

A deep breath filling his lungs, Mark Malloy laid aside his plate and rose from the edge of the bunk. "No need of my saying," he told the derelicts, "that I'm grateful for this. I didn't think there was much hope that you'd come, or that you'd even hear the signal."

"Sure we heard it. Sounded like a half dozen damn birds whistling down here. And when we saw all the Circle C beef and riding stock, we knew there must be something funny going on. Figured we owed it to you to sneak down and take a look, and see just why the hell you were calling us."

Tony Balter spoke up, then; face dark with rage, hands clenched on the edge of the table, he cried, "Wait a minute! Are you sayin' that—"

"That's just what he's sayin'!" interrupted the cook, his voice heavy with scorn. "Looks like Malloy is just one too many for you, Tony. This time you let him trick you into calling in help for him!"

Fury lifted Tony Balter out of his chair, whipping around toward the other man with a bellowed warning. "Keep your tongue or I'll—"

"You'll nothing!" snapped Malloy. "Quiet down, Tony, and let me take those guns that appear to give you so much trouble. Seems to me it's the second time I've had to do this."

The Circle C killer subsided, but he was a coiled spring of leashed, crazy destruction as the gambler walked up to him and lifted the weapons from his holsters, laying them on the table. Malloy then disarmed the other pair, in turn, and retrieved his .38 from the pocket of Ford's coat.

Ike said, "What are you going to do with them?"

"I'm thinking about it," said Malloy. "Where's your friend? Where's Lefty?"

"Outside. We left him to keep watch."

Malloy nodded. "Good enough! I'm expecting Pitt Caslon along, any minute—he'll figure I've walked into his trap by now, and that the sign is right to get that homestead title out of me. There'd likely have been a new cutbank grave up in the hills before morning," he added. "If you hadn't stepped in, that is!"

"Looked as though it might be something on that order," Ike agreed drily.

"Right now," continued Malloy in the same cold and emotionless tone, "there's one little matter I want to settle. But we'll do it outside—no point in smashing up the premises." He waggled his gunbarrel at the Circle C men. "After you, please!"

He ignored the bewildered looks that were given him as he herded his prisoners out of the cabin, picking up the lamp from the table in passing. Outside he thrust the lamp into the hands of big Ike, and then very deliberately he peeled out of his brush jacket and unstrapped his holster, and placed them in a neat pile, with his hat, on the corner of the stoop. The lamp, flickering in the shifting currents of the evening wind, cast oblique shadows across the planes of his face as he turned and sought out Tony Balter in the half circle of men around him.

He said, in a voice that held the tremor of anger, "You like to use your fists, don't you? Well, let's see you use them against a man who has a fair chance to fight back!" And he lashed out with a clubbed fist that glanced off Tony Balter's hard skull, and sent the man spinning to hit the ground full length.

Balter came bouncing up to his feet, instantly, as a gusty shout rose from the onlookers. Malloy heard one of them exclaim, "He's crazy! He can't lick Tony Balter!" As the Circle C killer started for him, and he measured himself against the size of the man, Mark Malloy conceded that this was probably right; but he was angry and the punishing blows he had taken from the big man still hurt. There were some things that a man could not accept without retaliation.

By then it was too late for caution, anyway, because Tony Balter had started for him with fists clubbed and swinging, and all the weight of his strong-muscled frame behind them.

His very first blow warned Malloy—if he hadn't had reason to know already—just what he was in for. He tried to step away from it but it landed against the point of one shoulder, with a force that felt almost enough to cripple it. He stumbled, caught his footing; he saw the next one coming and managed to block it, and then he found an opening and jabbed at the big man's body, aiming for the solar plexus.

There was the grunt of wind leaving the thick barrel of the man's chest and Balter had been stopped for an instant— long enough for Malloy to send a fist against the point of the hard, solid jaw. But his knuckles seemed to bounce off the craggy bone structure, like rubber; he was tiring, already, and he knew his arm did not have the weight for a knockout blow—not against an opponent of Balter's size and build.

Suddenly he was down, not sure how he had got there and aware only of the shock of pain. A bright blaze of light and heat was close to his face; he blinked against it, realizing that big Ike had set the lamp on the edge of the cabin stoop and that he had almost struck it in falling. As he fought to gather strength he heard Ike's yell of "Fair fight! Fair fight, damn you!" and, pushing against the edge of the stoop, rolled desperately away to escape Tony Balter's heavy cow-hide boots.

The flame of the lamp was burned into his vision now and he could, momentarily, see nothing. Blinking to drive away that smear of brightness dancing before him everywhere he looked, Mark Malloy got his feet under him. And Tony Balter was on him again, barely allowing him time to come fully to a stand. Malloy couldn't yet see his opponent; arcing fists rocked him, drove him back-pedaling across the uneven ground. But now his vision cleared a little and Balter showed as a vague, black outline against the dusk. He threw blows at this, reckless, forgetting all science. Then he was down again, as his knees lost their stiffness.

From a long way off, big Ike was yelling at him: "You damn fool! Why let him kill you?" It was a question that made sense. Resting there, on hands and knees, head hanging and blood dribbling from his nose into the dust, Mark Malloy wondered vaguely at himself. He who had never before know-ingly bucked a losing game—why should he stand up to the fists of Tony Balter and let himself be cut to ribbons, in the vain attempt to repay a couple of unfair blows?

These thoughts ran through his dazed mind. Then he ran a sleeve across his mouth, wiping away some of the blood, and lifted his head for a look about him—at the cleared space before the cabin, the dancing wash of light from the lamp on the stoop behind him, the trees and shouldering hills that rimmed this place. He saw Tony Balter, a little distance away, standing spreadlegged and panting as he waited; saw the excited, distorted faces of the watchers. And one other that he hadn't noticed, before that moment.

Yonder, at the edge of the circle, Pitt Caslon sat saddle with his hands piled on the horn and an arrogant and scorn-ful smile stamped upon his features. Malloy didn't know when the Circle C owner had ridden up, but he saw that the third outlaw, Lefty, had Caslon's silver-mounted .45; appar-ently the man had been taken prisoner easily enough. He spoke to Malloy, now, his harsh voice cutting across other sounds: "You keep biting off bigger chaws than you can handle, don't you, tinhorn?"

The muscles along Malloy's lower jaw bunched. He spat, flexed the fingers of his right hand hoping it wasn't broken. Then, doggedly, deliberately, he pulled himself to his feet and crouched that way as Tony Balter came in on him for the kill.

It was plain that the bully didn't know how this man—slight of build, untrained in rough-and-tumble—had stood up to him for even this long; but plainly, too, he thought that the end was close. He strode in confidently, building his blow and cocking it from the shoulder for a finish wallop that would stretch his enemy flat. He was perhaps a little too deliberate about it. He gave Malloy a second too long to get set for the blow, and when it came the gambler had managed to shift away from it, blocking it with a quickly raised elbow.

And then Malloy drove his own right fist straight into the center of Tony Balter's face, coming on to his toes to lay every pound of weight behind it. Pain ran like an electric shock up the length of his arm, and weakness made him stumble so that he had trouble catching his balance. But he had hurt Balter with that one.

Sobbing for breath, Malloy hurled his left after the other, reaching blindly for a target and feeling the solid impact as it connected. A clout on the side of the head shook him but it glanced off, missing its full force. He ducked, lunged forward and rammed his head into the chest of the other man. His right fist plowed into Balter's ribs and a left sank into the flat belly. He kept boring in like that, kept pushing, holding the slight advantage because he didn't dare let go of it. He himself was almost past feeling the punishment he took from his enemy.

And suddenly his fists met empty air, and checking himself before he stumbled and fell, Mark Malloy realized dully that Balter had dropped to the earth in front of him. Not unconscious—far from that; Malloy knew he lacked the sheer power of muscle to accomplish such a thing, and for a dazed moment he failed to understand. Raging with the fury that had broken all bounds within him, he stood over the huddled shape of his enemy and pawed at him, trying to grab hold somewhere and haul the man to his feet. "Get up!" he shouted, in a voice he hardly knew as his own. "On your feet and finish this!"

"Enough!" Unbelievably, that was Tony Balter's voice, shaken with pain and with something very close to fear, "I've had enough—"

Slowly, Mark Malloy straightened. He ran a look around at the faces that had suddenly gone silent and unmoving, and he dragged air into his bruised and battered body. He lifted a hand, ran it over his face, and looked at the blood; and then he put his stare on Pitt Caslon. Jabbing a thumb toward the figure huddled on the ground at his feet, he said hoarsely, "There he is, Caslon. There's your bully boy."

He was sore in every muscle and every limb; his shirt was torn, a ruin of blood and dirt and sweat. Turned suddenly weak with the aftermath of battle, he stumbled over to the wooden stoop before the cabin and sank down on the edge of it, and his shadow, made massive and grotesque by the lamp set so close beside him, spread blackly across the ground—the shadow of a man hunched and worn and panting.

The silence had been held, all that time. At last Mark Malloy lifted his head and swept back the hair which had tumbled into his eyes. "All right," he said, and his voice was tired. "Ike, you three all have guns now. As of right now you also have horses—good, Circle C riding stock. You'll find them in the corral; I make you a present of them, and these gents can walk home for all of me.

"I also make you a present of every head of Circle C beef stock that you find grazing on my quarter section. All you have to do is round them up and drive them off. Think you can find some place to get rid of them?"

Ike and Spud exchanged looks, and grins spread across their bearded faces. "Hell, yes!" said the leader of the three convicts. "With hosses under us there ain't anything we can't do. As for this beef stuff, we know of railroad construction camps back across the hills where they ain't particular who they buy their meat from."

"Get busy, then," said Malloy bluntly. "I don't want any of that stock left on my place come daylight. And you, Caslon, take these riders of yours—take them and get off my land. They'll have to walk to town; I suggest you let Tony Balter have the spare horse, because he's in poor shape for walking."

"Why, he can lie there and rot!" snarled Pitt Caslon. The Circle C owner was angry—beside himself at the turn things had taken here. He shouldered his big chestnut bronc forward and leaned from the chased leather saddle, the expensive gray sombrero masking his face as he glared down at his gunman in the dust.

"You hear me, Tony Balter?" he roared, in a tone of deep contempt. "You're fired! You had an easy job given you to do and you muffed it. Not only that, but you let this tinhorn work you over with his fists and crack you in two. He was beaten—out on his feet, done for—but when he started to hurt you, you caved like any yeller belly!" He spat, carefully and eloquently. "And that's Tony Balter—him that's had this whole range, and me too, thinkin' he was unbeatable! Well, you're finished, Tony. Don't stay around here. It'd make me sick, just lookin' at you!"

He straightened, glancing with contempt at Dick Ford and the other hand. "The same goes for the pair of you. I don't need your kind working for me. I can get other men—a single failure is all I have to allow for. Don't ride near Circle C again!"

Dick Ford cried, "But we got wages comin'!"

"Write me at the ranch after you get a hundred miles away from Hermit Flats; I'll see that they're mailed to you." Pitt Caslon looked at Mark Malloy for a second, as though he meant to add something. But then he changed his mind, and without another word touched steel to his horse. It was a high-strung animal; at the bite of the spur it leaped and then settled into a quick gait, and Pitt Caslon was gone into the shadows, swallowed up by the summer night, with the drum of his horse's hoofs quickly fading.

Big Ike turned on the dismissed Circle C hands. "Well," he grunted, "you see how it is. You're a long way from no-where, so you might as well start walking. Maybe you'll have to carry that big, tough hombre there on the ground."

"Damn you, shut up!" Tony Balter came lurching to his feet, screaming in a maddened frenzy. He would have hurled himself at the convict but the latter stepped back hastily, shoving the muzzle of his revolver into the killer's bloody face and halting him. Balter stood there, bullet head thrust forward, thick fingers working with rage. He had not really been hurt by Mark Malloy's fists; the gambler, looking at him, guessed this. What had broken Tony Balter was the surprise and terror at having a beaten enemy turn and carry the battle to him. It was a new thing for the bully, a thing his cruel and warped mind could not fathom. And it was this that had bested him.

Malloy understood that the man was no less dangerous than he had been before. In fact, his humiliation and dis-missal would have him stung to a greater deadliness than ever. And though Mark Malloy had beaten him in personal combat, he must remember he had never yet tried himself against the man's gunskill.

He slid the .38 from his holster, where it lay beside him on the neat pile of his brush jacket and hat, and he stood up a bit unsteadily as Tony Balter came whipping around, searching for him. Over the leveled gun Malloy said, "Enough for one night, Tony. I think you'd better get going. And I'm too tired to argue much about it."

"We'll settle this!" shouted the gunman, in his high-pitched voice. "You write that down somewhere and remem-ber it. Pitt Caslon can go to hell, if he wants to—but you, tinhorn, I'm sending personal!" He turned on Dick Ford and the other dismissed hand. "Come on! For now, let's get out of here!"

But the two exchanged a sullen look, and then turned their backs and started away, not waiting for him. It was a deliberate insult. The bully boy they had taken orders from in respect and awe had been dragged from his throne, shamed and humbled before their eyes; and now they were spurning him. The big man stared after them, plainly not understanding for a moment just what was happening. When the meaning of it came home to him his whole body jerked, as though to the impact of a physical blow.

But he said nothing more. He merely started after the other two, moving awkwardly in his peg-heeled boots, all emotion held and suppressed within his taut frame. And when the last sound of him had faded into the night, big Ike turned to his companions. "Well, let's get them broncs. We got beef to gather!"

"Only the Circle C horses," Malloy called as they headed at a run for the corral. "The bay is mine, and there's a couple of nags that belong to the livery—"

He would have to keep a watch on those horses tonight, he supposed, to prevent the three he had set afoot from circling back and trying to steal them out of the corral. Right now, he picked up the flickering lamp and his hat and jacket, and carried them inside the cabin and put them on the table. He stood looking about him dully for a moment; then he stumbled to the bunk and collapsed upon it, lay waiting dully for the strength and the will to do anything more.

15

A STEAMING SQUARE of sunlight, falling upon him through the open window, finally roused him. He lay as though drugged, unable to move. He had slept out the night and deep into the morning, without once changing position; and as a result his body held a cramped tiredness that only added to the soreness and fatigue of pounded muscles.

He levered himself off the bed, finally, and looked about him at the litter Circle C had left behind; the cabin, which he had kept scrupulously neat, appeared as though a tidying hand had never been put to work at it. He toed aside an empty whiskey bottle, went unsteadily to the table and pulled out a chair, slacked into it. He found room for his elbows amid the stacks of dirty tinware and leaned his head on his hands, waiting for the sluggish lethargy to pass.

As his head began to clear, Malloy found himself going back over the events of these last days, assessing the score and trying to decide where he now stood. He supposed he really hadn't done too badly. He had blocked every move by Pitt Caslon. He had broken Caslon's sheriff, and knocked two of the main props from under him by smashing Steve Wendell's gunarm, and thoroughly discrediting his most dangerous tool of all—the half-crazed Tony Balter. He didn't see how Caslon would be able to strike again until he had recouped these losses; which meant that Malloy could possibly expect a breathing spell. But for how long?

He touched his face, found dried blood in the stubble of a two-day beard, and raw places that caused him to wince beneath exploring fingers. From the bright world outside came the singing and twittering of birds, the run of a morning breeze through the treeheads; and behind them all, the steady music of the burbling spring. This latter sound, penetrating to the surface of Malloy's consciousness, locked his throat in a sudden, parching thirst. A cold, clean drag at that singing water was suddenly what he wanted above all else.

Pushing to his feet, he got an empty pail from its hook and went out into the sunlight, moving stiffly as he worked the soreness out of his limbs.

On the mossy edge of the spring he bellied flat and drank directly from its surface, sucking up the water. He sank his knuckle-swollen hands wrist deep and scooped up water and splashed it against his face, and the drops fell back reddened with blood. Blinking against the sting of it, he rolled to his knees and wiped his face carefully and gingerly on the tail of his shirt.

Afterwards, feeling clearer-headed because of the cold strike of the water, he rose, rinsed out his pail and filled it, and turned back again toward the cabin. He had covered half the distance when the gunshot sounded.

Three thoughts struck him, all in the same instant and all distinct and crystal clear: first, that he was caught out here in the open, a considerable distance from any cover; secondly, that he was unarmed—his .38 and the new rifle, both, having been left by unforgiveable carelessness within the shack; and thirdly, that the bullet could have killed him but had, instead, been aimed deliberately for the bucket in his hand.

He had felt the jerk of the heavy pail, as the lead skewered it. Now twin jets of water sprang from two holes bored neatly through the metal. Malloy tossed aside the ruined pail, and flung himself prone.

At once a second report split the echoes of the first, and dirt gouted up only inches from Malloy's head. He flinched away from it, panicky at the realization of his exposed position, while he had so far been unable to sort out the echoing racket of the gunfire and reach a judgment as to where his enemy or enemies might be. He was pinned there, helpless, not knowing in what direction he could hope to hunt a break for safety.

Then wild, high-pitched laughter came to him across the returning silence. "That's right, Malloy—crawl! Dig a hole in the dirt with your bare hands! I'll kill you when I'm ready!"

A third bullet showered him with rubble as it skewered the earth, this time placed on the other side of him to show that he was centered and that his tormentor could have finished him, easily, with any of his shots.

Malloy forced himself to hold steady while the dirt pattered around him, and afterwards lifted his head. He saw Tony Balter, then. The man had stepped into the open from behind a scrub oak, near the foot of the slope that backed the homestead. Hard to say how long he might have waited there for this chance at the man he hated; Malloy wondered if he had walked all the way to town to find a horse and a gun, so he could return and fulfil his crazed need for vengeance.

Bitterness and loathing were in the answer Malloy hurled back. "Go ahead, you butcher! You damned, crazy killer— who don't have the nerve to stand up to an equal chance!"

In reply, Balter worked the trigger again; and Malloy, for all his fierce determination not to grovel before the man, ducked quickly as the lead went by him—so close that he thought he felt the tap of concussion against his face. Tony Balter's laughter followed; he was taking the keenest sort of pleasure from this cruel game.

But he was not crazy enough to allow himself carelessness; and now, with only four shots emptied from his gun, he stopped to reload. Big shape braced on widespread boots, he kicked out the spent shells and began to stuff new brass into the cylinder.

He was perhaps ten yards from where Mark Malloy crouched helpless in the full beat of the sunlight. For a gunman of Balter's skill, this was not too far a range for accurate shooting; to Malloy, unarmed, it was a hopeless situation. Still, he could at least be man enough to go down fighting, and not wait here while the other baited him cruelly and finally, in his own good time, finished him with a bullet.

His jaw set hard, Mark Malloy pushed himself to his feet and started forward, crouched in an instinctive effort to make as small a target as possible.

At the first move, Tony Balter had rocked the cylinder back into place and brought the gun quickly into line again. "Coming to get it, are you?" he jeered. "I'll give it to you, all right—square between the eyes!" And he lifted the six-gun, and took a careful bead along its sights, his whole face twisted with concentration as he squinted at his victim.

Moving straight into the face of death, Malloy had a strange kaleidoscopic impression of many sights and impressions—thrown into a strange perspective and stamped, with sharp-etched clearness, upon his mind: an image of hill and trees and sky, an awareness of sunlight sparkling in unnatural brilliance on grass and bending treeheads, of the feel of the earth beneath his boots, of the song of wind and water and a camp robber's harsh scream somewhere in the timber. No doubt because this was likely his last minute on earth, some part of his mind was reaching out to grasp it all—greedy for everything that living meant and that was about to be snatched from him.

And, centering that odd medley of sensual images, was the shape of Tony Balter—the cropped black hair upon the hard skull, the mouth twisted in a wicked grin of pleasure—and, also, the black tunnel entrance which was the Colt's muzzle, pointing squarely at his face and ready at any instant to hurl death at him.

Then the voice of Jean Garrett cried: "Tony! Drop that gun! Drop it, you hear me?"

A convulsion appeared to shock its way through the man's body, causing his meaty shoulders and bullet-shaped head to jerk sharply. It was a wonder that his finger, crooked and hard against the trigger slack, didn't squeeze off the shot; had it done so—Malloy was himself too startled to move—the bullet would surely have killed him. But the shot didn't come. And now Jean Garrett repeated her warning, her voice holding a dangerous note of hysteria: "My rifle is aimed square between your shoulder blades, and I swear that if you don't drop that sixgun—"

Tony Balter wasn't too crazy to recognize real peril when he heard the threat of it. Slowly, as though it cost him a tremendous effort, he lowered the gun from its target. He looked at the weapon; his ugly face warped in an expression of fury and he threw the gun into the dirt, slamming it down hard.

That savage movement jarred Malloy out of a momentary, shocked inertia. He went running forward, on legs that trembled, and vaulting a down log climbed the short rise and leaned to scoop up the weapon Balter had discarded. And now Jean Garrett came into sight; her face was without color, and she held her shotgun braced against a hip, with hands that were white knuckled from the grip she had on barrel and buttplaces. Her eyes made a blue stain against the pallor of her face.

"It's all right," Malloy assured her quickly, finding his voice. "We've got his fangs pulled. He won't try anything."

Reaction hit her, now that the danger had passed, and she was trembling as she lowered the weapon. "I had never shot anyone," she said, in a muffled voice.

"Balter wouldn't have been a bad one to begin with!" He had time now to become angry, and looking at the ugly face of the one who had meant to kill him, he found himself hard put to maintain his control.

The mad eyes were slitted, the slash of a mouth quivering with the pent-up fury within the man. "I shouldn't of waited! I ought to know something always happens to save your damned, lucky hide for you! A trick—or somebody that butts in to cheat me of my chance." He cut his hot stare toward the girl. "You dirty little—"

"Don't say it!" Malloy snapped. "I'll slap it back into your teeth with your own gunbarrel!" As Balter subsided, he looked at the Colt in his hand; and then, deliberately, he opened the loading gate, shook the bullets out and threw them away in a glittering streak of sunlight on brass.

"So you've never had a decent chance at me?" he murmured. "Maybe you're right at that! Maybe this thing has gone too far, not to reach a settlement.

"Not here," he added quickly. "I have a team and rig to be returned to the livery stable in town. Tomorrow morning, at sunup, I'll be on the street in front of the hotel—the place where we first met, Tony! I guarantee no one will interfere. If you've got the guts to show, I'll be watching for you!"

He tossed the emptied gun in front of the other's boots. "Now, pick that up and take your horse, and get out of here!"

Their stares were locked, in a long exchange of hatred. Then, abruptly, Tony Balter leaned and swooped up the gun, and turning away tramped heavily off through the dappled tree shade. He had a horse tied, back there on the wooded slope. With Malloy carefully watching his movements, he whipped the reins free and lifted his heavy build into leather. He did not look back, he gave the horse an angry flailing with boot heel, and sent it buckjumping forward. He rode away through the timber, crashing in underbrush; quickly these sounds faded.

The girl said, "You shouldn't have let him go! He's crazy —and he's treacherous."

"He won't try to lay another ambush," Malloy told her, confidently. "He's got his own kind of pride. Since I've promised to meet him in the dust he'll hold off and keep that meeting."

"But do you think you stand any chance against him?"

"Does it matter to you, one way or the other?"

The thrust went home. He saw her breast lift to a quick intake of breath, saw strong white teeth catch at her lower lip.

She said, "Maybe you wonder, then, why I stopped him from killing you, just now. Maybe you wonder why I came over here."

"As a matter of fact," he said, remembering her manner toward him on the other occasions when they had met, "maybe I do."

"It's a fair question, I suppose. I've held a gun on you, and accused you of being a Caslon spy—of being something even worse than Tony Balter. And I said that, if I ever learned I was mistaken, I would have to come to you one day and—and—"

"Apologize?" he finished for her. "Yes, I remember. . . . And is that why you're here?"

It was costing her an effort, but she nodded. "If the news we've been hearing is true—about your defying Circle C, even being thrown into jail by Caslon. And now, after what I've just seen, I know for certain. I was completely wrong."

She was close to him her head lifted, her blue eyes troubled as they scanned his battered face. "You've been hurt! What have they done to you, Mark Malloy?"

"It's nothing." But when he tried to smile his sore cheek stretched and stung, painfully. Jean Garrett saw this reflected in his eyes and, with an impulse to compassion, lifted a hand and laid it on his arm.

His next move was without premeditation, and without excuse except that the ordeal of facing death a moment before had weakened his control, upset the delicate balance of his rational nature. Something went through him, as the touch of the girl lay upon his arm. Another moment, and his hands went out, seizing her; he pulled her close, and pressed his mouth against her own.

Taken by surprise, the thing was done before she could begin to struggle. But then she was fighting him, striking and kicking, and at last he had to set her free. She stumbled away, her face gone scarlet, her eyes bright with anger. She ran a hand across her mouth, across her cheek where his beard had scratched her. Then, spotting the shotgun that had fallen from her hand, she spun and stooped to snatch it up, her black curls swirling.

Malloy stood the way he was, hands at his sides. There seemed nothing he could say. He watched the shotgun lift in the girl's trembling hands, heard the blazing fury in her voice. "You're very sure of yourself, aren't you? I'm not so certain now that I care what happens tomorrow morning! It doesn't matter to me if Tony Balter kills you, or—"

She whirled, and left him. Malloy found his voice and cried: "Please! I'm sorry as hell, Jean. . . ." He knew, however, that he couldn't call her back.

He stood where he was, for long moments after she had mounted her pony and ridden away from that place. And when he turned slowly back toward the cabin, a kind of self-disgust—a species of emotion that was rare indeed with Mark Malloy—sat heavily upon him.

16

Even after a full twenty-four hours' resting, Malloy hadn't yet recuperated, entirely, from the punishment of Tony Balter's mauling fists. Stiff and sore in every muscle, he tooled his rented rig in under the low doorway of the public stable, wrapped the lines and with something of an effort swung down the hub of the wheel.

He paid little attention to the man to whom he paid hire for the team and wagon and gave over his bay gelding for the night, though the other was boggle eyed and bursting with talk about the events of these last days. Rumor had it, he said, that there had been a blow-up at Circle C; that Tony Balter himself had been among the riders dismissed out-of-hand. That no one cared to guess what Pitt Caslon had next in mind, although the affair of the stranger at Indian Springs was the subject of rampant discussion in every bar and bunk house on the Flats. The barnman had a lot of questions, but Malloy tossed him his money with hardly more than a glance and left him, curiosity unsatisfied.

As on the afternoon of his first coming to Hermit Flats, Mark Malloy walked along the hard-packed dirt of the pathway paralleling the wide and dusty street, where false fronts threw their long shadows. The heat of the day had begun to thin out a little, with the sun's descending. He went, as on that day, directly to the hotel and signed for a room for the night. The clerk, as curious as the man at the barn, said, "Leaving town or something, Mr. Malloy?"

"Not that I know of." Malloy held out his hand for the key, his expression cold and uninviting, and the clerk quickly reached one from the board and passed it over.

"Same room, Mr. Malloy. You found that one comfortable, didn't you?"

"It was all right."

He had turned away and nearly reached the stairs when the clerk, for once, said something which held interest for him: "I understand Pitt Caslon is in town."

This was news, and Malloy stopped and looked at the man for a second, considering it. Then he shrugged, thinking, *I don't look for trouble with Caslon but I'm not running away from it*. And he went up the creaking stairs and to his room, where he stripped down and washed the dust of the Flats from his face and upper body.

He gave himself a long scrutiny in the glass, frowning at the marks of Tony Balter's fists. The cuts and bruises, still sore and stinging from the dust and the soap and the rough towel, and the blurred contours of his features where the skin was puffy and swollen, made him shake his head ruefully. "Whatever happens, you aren't going very soon to forget Tony Balter. You'll be reminded of him every time you look at the ruin of yourself in the glass!" But in time, he supposed, the marks would disappear; and he hoped they wouldn't leave any permanent disfigurement.

Finished here, he left the door unlocked and went down again to the street, and to a restaurant where he ordered supper. It was the third eating place he had sampled in this town and it was no improvement over the other two; but bad as the food was, he was used to restaurant cooking and it was better than his own. He took his time with the meal. Stars were out when he left the eat shack and walked slowly back to the hotel, lighting an after-dinner cheroot.

So far he had seen no sign of Pitt Caslon or any Circle C rider.

In the hotel bar he had a shot of rye, and decided the liquor here was not as bad as Frank Downing had led him to expect. He went out to the veranda and stood a while at the edge of the steps, teetering on his heels and working at the cigar as he admired the starry, lamp-splashed night. But he was tired and a good rest seemed in order, for he must be up before dawn. He was reflecting on the profound changes his habits of life had undergone, during this brief time on the Flats, as he pitched his cigar butt over the railing and went inside the hotel and up to his room.

Groping in the dark, he found the round center table and the lamp that hung above it, and struck a light. He was adjusting the glass shade when the voice behind him said, "Hello, tinhorn!" There was the sharp click of a gunsear.

Caught like that, both hands raised to the overhead lamp, he could not have gone for a gun even if he had wanted to take the risk. He might, of course, have put out the light and taken a drop to the floor, but a single bullet could finish him in the time it would require to do that. So instead he deliberately finished his job with the lamp, and then he turned slowly, hands still lifted, and looked into the truculent, square-jawed face of Pitt Caslon, and at the gun in Caslon's hand.

The Circle C boss sat in a tilted-back chair, against the wall by the door. He said now, "Didn't know whether you were coming back to your room or not, tinhorn. We been waitin' here quite a piece for you." He gestured with the muzzle of the naked gun. "These three are my new riders, Malloy."

Then Malloy saw the others, all armed, all watching him wordlessly. He recognized them in some astonishment. The big man leaning his shoulders against the wall on the opposite side of the door was the convict, Ike. That was Spud who hunkered near him, toying idly with a revolver, spinning it by its trigger guard. Lefty was the one stretched comfortably on the bed, a twisted grin on his wizened face as he blinked at Malloy in the lamp's sudden brightness.

Malloy couldn't say anything for a moment, digesting this. He noted considerable change in the three chain-gang fugitives. For one thing, they were shaven and cleaned up, and they had got rid of their hodge-podge of misfit riding clothes and prison garb; their boots were new and shiny in the lamplight, their jeans and work shirts fitted them, and they all had gleaming new gunharness strapped around their middles.

"Well," grunted Malloy, "you boys have come up in the world, haven't you? Must have sold that Circle C beef for a nice figure."

Pitt Caslon shook his massive head. "No," he answered the gambler. "These fellows are working for me now, taking the place of Tony Balter and the other pair I had to fire. Make good hands, too. They saw the sense of taking my proposition, when I caught up with them on the trail to the construction camps and put it to them."

Slowly, Malloy ran a level glance from one to the other of the trio, and at something in his eyes their own wavered a little, uneasily. "So it was your own selves that you sold!" Malloy said, finally.

Big Ike straightened up, pulling his shoulders away from the wall. "Hell!" he muttered, belligerently. "We'll deal with the highest bidder, any week. And Caslon had a lot more than gunwages to offer. Remember, it's his sheriff we been running from. Well, now we ain't running. As long as we take Circle C orders, this is one range where we can ride open and free and know that no law is gonna nab us and put back on the chain!"

Malloy considered, and he nodded slowly. "I guess I see your point. Yes, from your way of looking at it, I suppose that was a bargain you couldn't afford to miss." He looked at Pitt Caslon. "Well, it's your party. Let's get on with it."

The Circle C boss let the legs of his chair down, without noise, and moved ponderously to his feet. His hard mouth quirked beneath the roached mustache, the gun held level in his bronzed fist. "You're a nervy rooster, and a game one," he said, grudgingly. "Too bad you have to be a damn fool on top of it. . . . You figure yourself for a gambler, do you?"

"I like the name better than 'tinhorn,'" Malloy answered with a shrug.

"Well, maybe we'll just find out how good you are. That's why I'm here, mister. It's a hell of a time since I've sat in on a decent game of cards. Now, you're going to show me if you can bluff me at poker as easily as you've bluffed me for every foot of Indian Springs." He jabbed a thumb at the round center table, under the lamp. "That'll do for a table. Here's cards." He dragged a pack from his coat pocket, tossed them out under the cone of yellow light.

Malloy frowned in disbelief. "You're serious about this? You've tracked me here, just to call for a game of cards? And for what stakes?"

"For all of them! No ceiling—no limit. I could take Indian Springs at the point of this gun, mister; instead, I'm gonna beat you, and beat you for keeps—at your own game!"

"And after that?"

"I don't give a damn! You'll be free to ride off these Flats —busted—and no Circle C rider will lift a hand to stop you. But that's after I break you, Malloy. In this room—over this table. Where nobody can interrupt us until the job is done!"

Mark Malloy looked around him, slowly comprehending that the Circle C boss meant every word he said. The pride of Pitt Caslon had been badly treated since the arrival of the stranger; this, seemingly, was the only way in which he thought he could find a fitting retribution. And obviously he was going to have his chance, because there could be no arguing against a drawn gun, and the guns of these three new riders of his.

Malloy read no compromise in the faces of Ike and the others; once, they had sided with him, briefly, but now such loyalty as they possessed belonged entirely to the man who paid them wages, and gave them the protection of his crooked law machine. Mark Malloy could expect no help from that quarter—or no mercy, either, if it came to that.

He lifted his shoulders, in a shrug. "I'm tired as the devil. I meant to get to bed early. But you're running the show."

"Damn right I am. Ike—Spud!" Caslon snapped his fingers, and the men leaped into action, clearing the table, getting ready. Caslon stepped over to his prisoner, snaked the .38 revolver from Malloy's underarm holster and tossed it on the bed; then, and then only, he shoved his own gun into the metal-studded Mexican holster belt at his stocky waist.

"You look a sight worse than tired," he went on, studying

Malloy's battered face with evident amusement. "Which reminds me, I've heard talk that Tony Balter didn't leave, the
way I told him. They say he's still around—that he means
to settle with you before he gits. Heard anything to that
effect?" And when Malloy made no answer: "Well, anyhow,
that's why I'm taking care of my score with you tonight,
before he's had his chance. Because, I don't think you can
whip Tony in a stand-up gunduel in the dust. My bets are
all the other way, on *that* game!"

The other refused to show in any way how this taunting
affected him. Face expressionless, he pulled back one of the
chairs Ike had placed at the table and seated himself under
the cone of the overhead lamp, his lean fingers picking up
the box of cards and quickly breaking the seal. The slick
pasteboards came into his hand like old and familiar friends,
after these weeks of separation from his profession. Malloy
riffled them, shuffled, the red backs of the cards flashing
brightly.

He looked around. "Well, let's get this started," he said
shortly.

Enough chairs had been rounded up somewhere—probably
by ransacking other rooms of the hotel—to seat all five of
them. The convict, Lefty, said dubiously, "I don't belong in
any cutthroat game like this is gonna be. I'll watch."

"You'll play," Caslon told him, flatly. "I'm in the mood
for a little friendly poker, first, to get the ball rolling—and
five-handed is the best kind." He lowered his stocky frame
into the chair opposite Malloy's and without further com-
ments the three new Circle C hands took their places. Caslon
brought a roll of greenbacks from his pockets and dropped
them in front of him. "Table stakes," he said. "Deal, Malloy."

The cards flickered under the lamp, as the gambler's slim
fingers began to pass them out, five around.

At first the game went quietly indeed, no one winning or
losing in any great amount; Malloy decided the Circle C
boss was studying him, taking his measure before opening

up with all the big guns. And Malloy had no objection to this, for it gave him time to ease into the thing.

Skill and training such as Malloy's could not be much dulled in a period of less than a month, but on the other hand he realized at once that he was not in his best form. He was logy with tiredness and the aftermath of his beating. As the hours dragged out, with small winnings moving back and forth and the tide not setting strongly in any one direction, he found difficulty in holding attention on the cards, on his fellow players, on the drift of small talk. And he noted with alarm that his eyes were again beginning to smart in the smoky air and the lamplight.

It was midnight or shortly afterwards that he realized he was losing, steadily, and that the money was dwindling from the stack on the table's edge in front of him.

This thought stabbed home suddenly and it hauled him out of a kind of somnolence that had fallen over his fatigued brain. He lost a sizeable pot that he should have won, and as he watched the convict, Spud, rake his money in he took warning with the thought, *The pressure is starting. Wake up, fellow, and on your toes!*

He put a narrow surveillance on the other players and on the cards that passed through his fingers, meanwhile holding back sharply on his betting until he could discover where the trouble lay. It did not take him long. His sensitive finger tips quickly detected what he ought to have noticed before: Someone had been using his thumbnail to mark the backs of the cards.

It was one of the easiest and oldest methods of trickery in the business—but who was doing it? As Malloy tossed in the cards for the deal, he thoughtfully considered the other players, reconstructing the pattern of recent hands. Just now, Spud had been the winner; but he hadn't dealt, and only the dealer has any advantage when the pasteboards are marked for touch. Of course, it could be that all four of his opponents were rigging the game against him. Still, he had to know for sure. And the method of finding out was simple enough.

He merely began altering, with his own fingernail, the

markings on all the cards that passed through his hands. And sure enough, after a while, the playing began to go slightly awry, and he saw a look of growing puzzlement begin to deepen on Pitt Caslon's blocky, arrogant face. Malloy read nothing similar in the expressions of the others; this satisfied him that Caslon had been alone in the crookedness and that only he found things going wrong now. The matter came to a head finally when, on Caslon's deal, Malloy drew a good hand and won with it, and the Circle C owner, who had bet high on cards of his own, cursed explosively and slammed the deck into the middle of the table.

"I agree with you," said Malloy, eyeing the other mildly. "We ought to have new cards. The backs of these are getting all scratched up. . . ."

Caslon's head jerked and as he read Malloy's meaning his broad face began to color. For a moment they stared at each other, understanding perfectly how things stood between them. Then Caslon turned to hurl an order at the leader of the convicts. "Go down to the bar, Ike. Get another pack, and bring up a bottle and glasses with you."

There was a brief break while the man was gone. Pitt Caslon rose heavily, moved to the window and running up the shade leaned out for a look upon this sleeping town of Hermit Flats—*his* town. Utter stillness came into the stuffy room, carried on the refreshing night wind that stirred drifting layers of blue cigar smoke. Two o'clock, Malloy thought.

Let down by this break in the steady concentration of playing, he felt the rush of tiredness possess him. He placed his elbows on the table, and pressed the heels of his palms across his closed eyes. Pain shot through them—that old sensation of feeling as though his eyes were filled with particles of sharp sand. When he took the hands away, he was left blinking at the stab of the lamp glare.

He thought, *Doc Reading and his rest cure! My eyes are every bit as bad as they've ever been!*

Then Ike had returned, clinking a bar bottle and a handful of glasses. Pitt Caslon drew the window shade again and returned to his chair, and while Lefty began to shuffle the new deck of cards he pulled the cork of the bottle, poured drinks. He started to shove a glass to Malloy, but the latter shook his head.

The hard mouth below Caslon's roached mustache quirked. "Playing cagey?" he grunted. "A good idea, tinhorn. I've been going easy, up to this. But it's getting late. Starting now, I'm coming after you!"

"Good luck," said Malloy drily. "But forget that thumbnail trick, will you? It'll just get you into trouble."

Caslon smirked. "Don't worry about me! You watch out for your own hide."

"It's fastened on pretty tight," said Malloy, and reached for his cards.

At once, the tempo of the game, the very atmosphere of the smoky room, seemed to undergo a change. Pitt Caslon was angry, and now he was out for blood. Malloy could feel the mounting pressure against him.

He began to slip behind, rapidly. Caslon, he commenced to realize, was one who possessed a fairly large pack of crooked tricks and was fairly competent at playing them. He used the holdout, the card switch, and the palmed card. He dealt off the bottom, and he dealt the second card and even on occasion the third from the top. He fake-shuffled and fake-cut. And he altered his technique so expertly that Malloy—familiar as he was with all these tricks—was not always sufficiently quick at detecting what his opponent was up to and preparing his strategy of defense.

He was considerably surprised at such skill in the man— and such blatant use of it, from one who had taken special delight in goading Malloy himself with the unpleasant name of "tinhorn." Scorn and anger rose in the gambler, as he thought of that. He fought his emotions back, because his wits—drugged as they were by tiredness—had to be at their sharpest edge and free from such blinding hindrances. His eyes were already tormenting him, almost past concentration on the cards.

Suddenly Caslon slammed down the shot glass he had just drained, and turned on his three henchmen. "Enough of this!" he declared loudly. "The game's over, as far as you three are concerned. There'll be one more hand—showdown, Malloy, between you and me. You understand? The stakes will be the title to Indian Springs. Put it on the table!" And he himself lifted his silvermounted .45 revolver out of the Mexican holster, and placed it in front of him, near his hand.

Malloy looked at the gun. He looked at Caslon's craggy features and then at the three convicts, who were quietly pushing back their chairs obedient to their employer's order to get out of this game. As Caslon had said, this was showdown; and there was no avoiding it.

A tiny, jeweled drop of liquor glimmered on the table top in front of the Circle C boss. Malloy had watched him spill it there, carefully; he was using it every time he dealt, a mirror in which he could see reflected the face of each card as he slid it from the pack. Such familiar trickery had Caslon resorted to, blatantly; yet against it Malloy had played clean poker, knowing that a single slip on his part would be the signal Caslon had been waiting for—the excuse to drag his gun and shoot the gambler where he sat.

Now, however, he had come to the end of that road. It was the moment for daring, and he had already decided what course he was going to take.

He said, "What are you putting up against my bet? That gun?"

"What difference does it make to you?" retorted Caslon. "This is one hand you aren't going to win!"

"You seem pretty sure. Let's see just how sure!" And opening the front of his shirt, Mark Malloy dragged out the money belt containing his sacred, last-stake reserve of cash. Without any sign of what it meant to him to do it, he tossed the belt into the center of the table. It landed with a solid thump, indicating the sizeable amount contained in its canvas pockets; and taking the patent to Indian Springs from his coat, Malloy placed it beside the belt.

"That's the works," he said. "That, and my bay gelding down in a stall at the livery. Every cent and everything I own is in this pot, Caslon. Let's see you equal it. Let's see you put Circle C on the block, against this!"

Pitt Caslon turned a darker color. "Why damn you, what do you take me for? I don't care how much you got in that stinkin' money belt—it couldn't touch a tenth of what Circle C is worth!"

Malloy cocked an eyebrow. "Oh, getting scared? You think now you might not win this hand, after all?"

His goading had its effect. "You've got a bet!" roared Caslon, dropping the weight of a meaty hand flat upon the table. He grabbed the half-empty bottle, sloshed liquor into his glass and downed the drink with a toss of his solid, blocky head. "Shoot the works—and I warn you, if you try any crooked playing it will be the last hand you ever play. You understand?"

"Certainly," answered Malloy, smiling. He glanced at the three convicts. "You're my witnesses. He made the bet—everything he owns, against everything I own. That agreed?"

"Sure," said Ike heavily. "We heard him."

Pitt Caslon growled, "Cut the cards!" And nodding his satisfaction, Mark Malloy reached and with all their eyes on his deft movements, performed that operation.

When he withdrew his hand, the card from the top of the pile was fitted snugly and unsuspectedly into the curve of the fingers. He transferred this card to his sleeve, for safe keeping, and then sat back patiently to wait while Pitt Caslon began his deal.

17

Pɪᴛᴛ Cᴀsʟᴏɴ wᴀs by no means drunk, but he had taken on enough liquor to blur his movements and render his hand just a bit unsteady—enough, at any rate, that his misdealing of the cards was all too poorly concealed. Mark Malloy had to sit there while he fumbled with the deck, squinting at the spots reflected in the drop of whiskey, painstakingly choosing the hands he wanted to give himself and his opponent.

Such cheating was so obvious that no tyro could have missed it. Malloy observed it all in silence, and then, as he reached to pick up his cards, he caught big Ike's attention and he gave the man a nod and a wink. It was all the gesture he needed to make. It took the big man into his confidence, briefly, and shared with him a secret joke at Caslon's clumsy cheating. Ike seemed to find small amusement in it, however. He dropped his eyes, scowling—almost as though with shame for the man who was his chief.

Satisfied with these results, Malloy fanned his cards and studied them, frowning a little. God, his eyes hurt! The left one was watering slightly, smearing his vision. He blinked to clear it. He was holding about what he had expected Caslon would give him—a low pair, just good enough cards that he might be lulled into thinking the deal had been an honest one. Caslon, probably, was sitting there with nothing less than a full house—and very smug in his confidence of victory.

Quietly, Malloy shook the hold card out of his sleeve and exchanged it for one from his hand—all done so expertly that none of the four men observing him could possibly have detected a hint of what he was up to. The card he had palmed from the deck was a nondescript seven of spades—it served his purpose completely.

Pitt Caslon was leering at him across the table. "You want any cards, tinhorn?"

"I'll take a couple," said Malloy, and picked his discards from his hand. One of these was the seven of spades—and it was his card which, in tossing them down, he managed by a carefully contrived accident to drop face upward, briefly. "Sorry!" he grunted, and flipped it over and shoved it into the discard.

He picked up the two Pitt Caslon had already peeled off the deck for him, fitted them into his hand. Only then did he glance up, and see the thunderous look on the face of the Circle C boss.

"Something wrong?" he asked, mildly.

"You crook!" Caslon was on his feet, his voice a hoarse croak of fury. "You dirty, cheating tinhorn—"

"What are you raving about?" Malloy cut in on him. "I'm ready for a show of cards. Are you afraid to go through with it?"

For answer, Caslon slapped his cards violently into the discard, face down. "I'm not callin' your hand!" he shouted. "I'll put a bullet through your guts first. You was warned what to expect if you tried a phony play."

"Every card I hold is one you dealt me," said Malloy, and he spread them out—a pair of nines, a deuce, a five, and one lone Ace. *"Do you deny it?"* His voice snapped a challenge, before which Pitt Caslon could only shake his head a little, staring at the hand without comprehension.

"But that—that seven of spades you burned—"

"Discarding isn't playing," Malloy reminded him. "And while we're on the subject of cheating—isn't it a bit peculiar you should know just what you dealt me?"

The words were quiet enough, but they held a prod that all at once stung Pitt Caslon to a killing frenzy. "Damn you!" he screamed. And with face twisted in hatred, he grabbed up the gun from the table and dropped it into line against the unarmed man seated across from him. The hammer rose.

Big Ike said, "You've gone far enough, Caslon. Drop it!"

Slowly, unbelieving, the Circle C boss turned until he was staring into the barrel of the gun the convict had leveled at him. For a long moment no one moved or spoke; then big Ike repeated, "Drop the gun!" And it fell from Caslon's hand, thudding on the table.

"I still got a little self-respect left," big Ike said, heavily. "Enough that I cannot stomach any more of this. I've sat here tonight and watched you perform, Pitt Caslon, until I was ashamed to be drawing your wages; but this is the end, as far as I'm concerned."

The Circle C boss found words, then—scathing, scornful ones. "Why, you dumb chain-gang rat! I give you the chance of your life, and look what you've done with it. Well, you're through on this range, as of right now!"

"Oh, no! I think *you're* the one that's through. You made a bet with Malloy—remember? Circle C, and all the rest. You bet, but you didn't call his hand. And that means—at least, the way I always played poker—that you lose this pot. Am I right, boys?"

He appealed for confirmation to his fellows. Lefty and Spud exchanged a look, and then slowly they nodded. "That's poker," said Spud. "The Hoyle brand."

It took a moment yet for Caslon to realize just what was happening. When he did he turned white and then red; he started trembling so that he had to grip the edge of the table, leaning across it to shout directly into the face of big Ike. "You traitor! You can't bluff me. You can't railroad me into anything!"

"I'm not bluffing," said Ike. He raised his gun. "Before you leave this room, brother—*if* you leave it—you're going to pay off your debt. You're going to sign over to this gent full title to every foot of property you own on Hermit Flats. And me and the boys will witness it."

"You can't witness anything!" Pitt Caslon screamed.

"You're a set of two-bit jailbirds and without my protection you'll be back on the chain gang within a week!"

Ike rubbed his cheek with the knuckles of one hand. "Oh, I don't reckon. We got horses, and we'll have a head start on the law. In a month we'll be so far from here they'll never find us. It looked for a while like a good setup with you, Mr. Caslon, but the more we see of it the more we think we'd like Mexico better. That the way you boys feel about it?"

"We're with you, Ike," Lefty agreed. "You've always been the brains of our combination."

"And if our signatures ain't good enough, Mr. Caslon, why, there's a lawyer right across the street. Getting pretty close to daylight. We'll just take you over there and let him witness this deal between you and Malloy, and see that it's all legal and proper."

"Daylight?" echoed Malloy suddenly, his first word during this exchange between the convict and the Circle C boss. He rose quickly, strode to the window and flicked up the shade. A wide banner of sunrise colors flaunted its brilliance in the pale sky of morning, far across the wide Flats and the tawdry buildings of the town. The high court-house cupola was already gilded by the sun that stood, red and swollen, at the very rim of the horizon.

Mark Malloy looked out upon the morning. It was not the first time he had sat at a poker table throughout the length of a night and risen as day came upon the world; but never before had he played for such stakes, or with death sitting at his elbow, and never had he turned defeat to improbable victory by such a narrowly calculated decision about men and their reactions.

He turned back into the room, and found the eyes of all four upon him, Pitt Caslon slumped into his chair as though stunned and only now crediting the full force of his defeat. Malloy looked at him, and he looked at the trio of convicts. "Thanks," he said heavily. "It looked as though I was sunk, for a while."

It was all he needed to say. He walked to the table, took the Indian Springs patent and put it in his coat. He picked up the pack of cards and shaped it in his lean fingers, frowning. Somehow he knew that, whatever followed now, this long night just passed was the turning point with him. The stakes for which he had fought had given him all he needed of card playing, for a lifetime. He wanted no more. He was not any longer a gambling man.

With this strange knowledge that it was for the last time, he split the deck and turned up to see what he had cut. The Ace of spades—the card of death. He tossed the deck aside.

Taking from the table the loaded money belt which for so many years had been with him a fetish—the superstitious symbol of his gambler's luck—he weighted it in his hand, and then with a shrug of indifference tossed the belt over to the convict, Ike. "That's for you," he said. "Split it among you, with my compliments. There's just one other thing you can do for me."

"Name it!" said Ike, grinning at the heft of the money belt.

"Keep an eye on our friend Caslon, here, for a few minutes. I'll just step across to Downing's office and fetch the lawyer back here with me, to witness the deed to Circle C. After that, you're free to go anywhere or do anything you like."

"We'll keep him," Ike promised.

Malloy glanced at the beaten Pitt Caslon, but the man was staring brokenly at nothing, his craggy face bereft now of all its arrogant truculence, looking somehow out of shape. Not speaking to him, Malloy got his .38 from the bed and put it into the shoulder holster. Then he left that room where the low-burning lamp still vied weakly with strengthening daylight.

He went down through the silent hotel building, moving under a heavy weight of drugged tiredness, and out upon the veranda—and here the first level rays of the sun hit him with a sudden, golden-bright dazzle.

Stopping in his tracks, instantly blinded, Malloy jerked to avert his gaze from that stabbing punishment. He lifted a hand to his tortured eyes, blinking against the tears that quickly flooded them. This moment of agony was his ultimate reward—the moment of which Doc Reading had been warning him when he said, "These all-night sessions will finish you!"

For it was just then that the voice of Tony Balter lifted across the stillness of the street. "All right, Malloy," he cried in a high-pitched yell of hatred. "This is it. I'm waiting here to kill you!"

Desperately Mark Malloy blinked and pawed at his tortured eyes, tying to clear them. A bloodshot haze lay over everything, a fuzzy nimbus obscuring the outlines of every object; and when he sought to locate his enemy, he realized that Tony Balter stood in shadow at the opposite side of the street, where the light had not yet touched, while he himself was limned in the direct blast of the sun shining full against him. It made an impossible setup.

But he kept his head, knowing he couldn't sidestep this, and he forced an iron control on leaping nerves. Tilting his head sharply, he found, brought the narrow shadow of his hatbrim down across his eyes and, by squinting, he could just make out dimly the bulky figure of the gunman standing before the door of a building across the wide thoroughfare. He put his whole attention on this, knowing if he lost his target he might not find it again. And doing so, he started moving down the steps and into the street—deliberately, without haste but hoping to be able to cross that dividing line of shadow before the gunplay started. If he could only get that sun out of his face his small chances would be vastly improved.

He felt the hard dirt of the path under his boots, and then the edge of the rutted roadway. He picked his footing cautiously, not daring a stumble on the ruts. Yonder, it seemed to him the bulky shape of Tony Balter had changed slightly; the man had pulled himself into a more compact outline, crouching a little with his bullet head settled deeper between hunched shoulders. He was in a killer's stance, waiting, letting his enemy come to him. Malloy could not see his face, would not be able to read in it any of the telltale signs by which a gunman signals his draw before he makes it. His own right arm was lifted, elbow crooked, slim hand cocked to slide with all possible speed into the gap of his coat. But he counted his odds and found them poor indeed.

Then a woman's screams shrilled across the quiet, making taut nerves leap and pulling his eyes momentarily off their target. He caught a brief glimpse of Jean Garrett, astride her chestnut mare with the Star 7 hand, Nat Huber, beside her; they had ridden into the street from the north trail and had hauled rein as realization of what was shaping here struck them and tore the involuntary cry from the girl. Malloy wanted to yell at her to send her back out of the danger of wild bullets, but his voice caught in a dry throat.

In that same brief glance, too, he noticed a head thrust from a window above the street—saw that it was Frank Downing, staring at the scene below, unmoving. No doubt there were other witnesses to see him die in front of Tony Balter's sure and deadly guns.

But he put these others from his mind, and, blinking his smarting eyes for clearer vision, sought again for his enemy as he took another pace forward, and another. The edge of the shadow lay now not two yards ahead of him. Once beyond that, his chances would double.

It was at this moment that Tony Balter made his draw.

At the last, there was a hint of warning after all. Tony Balter had a shoulder hitch, that pulled his body into an odd shape the fraction of a second before his hands dived for holstered guns. Malloy caught this movement and he interpreted it rightly—even without Jean Garrett's quick cry of "Mark! *Look out!*" And as the killer's weapons cleared leather he was whipping out his own .38 revolver, at the same moment hurling himself bodily forward.

18

A GUN'S VOICE smashed the taut silence to pieces. The shock Malloy felt, however, was not that of a bullet striking him, but of his body hitting the dirt in a rolling sprawl. And now at last he was in shadow, the low sun gone from his eyes; and lying there on his side he found he could make out his enemy quite distinctly through the drift of stirred dust.

Tony Balter shot a second time, and dirt kicked and showered the prone man's body. He retained that iron grip on himself, however, bringing his light-framed .38 up and forward at arm's length, his eyes finding the faint gleam of sights and trying to lay this accurately against the shape of Balter before he hit trigger.

But dust had got into his burning eyes and the target began to swim before them, as they filled with unbidden tears. Cursing, gritting his teeth, Malloy blinked desperately; it was almost a blind shot he took, even as one of Balter's weapons thundered yet another time.

Desperately he fired, and fired again—as rapidly as he could work the trigger. The mingling of the explosions, the sharp sting of cordite, seemed to combine to form a moment with no beginning and no end. And through it all he thought he heard, repeated, Jean Garrett's shrill scream of terror.

Then something drove a hot lance deep into his shoulder. He gasped, sickened with the pain. He tried to keep shooting but the .38 was all at once too heavy a weight for his wrist. And though the racket of the guns had ceased, for long moments, Malloy's shocked brain could not seem to register the fact.

Dazed, he realized then that the fight was over and that he was still alive. He got an elbow against the ground, pushed to a sitting position.

And yonder lay Tony Balter, face down, arms flung wide and his twin guns smoking beside him.

Astonishment shocked through Malloy, as he understood the improbable thing that he had accomplished. But then his blurred glance lifted to the windows of Frank Downing's office and seeing the lawyer outlined there he thought, grimly, *This is a good time to finish all the odd jobs!* The decision got him onto his feet, a little unsteady and with the hurt shoulder throbbing badly. He walked over to Tony Balter's lifeless form, stood looking at him a moment as he ran a sleeve of his ruined coat across his face, swabbing away the dust and sweat. His eyes weren't bothering him quite so much as they had a moment ago.

He turned away, then, and headed for the store building. Jean Garrett and the Star 7 rider had had a little trouble with their horses during the shooting, but they had them quieted now and, as Malloy went past, the girl came down from saddle, calling his name. "A minute," he said and, ignoring the townsmen who were already spilling out upon the street in the wake of the excitement, he turned and swung up the rickety outside stairs to the door of Downing's office, smoking .38 still in his hand.

Downing opened to him, dressed only in pants and shoes and half-buttoned shirt; his hair was wild and his lean, sardonic face even more pallid than usual. "You did it!" he exclaimed, self-composure broken before his excitement. "You downed Tony Balter! I wouldn't have believed, if I hadn't seen—"

Shoving through the door, Malloy took the knob out of Downing's hand and slammed the door, faced the lawyer in the gloom of the dingy office. The other's expression altered a little at something he read in the face of his visitor. He said, trying to conceal his doubt, "Something I can do for you, friend? A drink, maybe—to brace you after what you've just been through?"

"No drink," said Malloy flatly. "There's a job waiting for you, in my hotel room across the street. A signature to be witnessed and notarized. And there's one other thing, before we go."

"Name it."

The gun in Malloy's hand snapped level. "The money," he said. "The ten thousand belonging to Ben Garrett and his daughter. I'll take that."

The eyes widened, the cynical mouth lost its shape as the words hit home. Frank Downing tried to make a quick recovery, but he could only stammer, "I don't—I don't think I know what you're talking about!"

"I think you do. That ten thousand disappeared right here in your office, during the excitement when Pitt Caslon broke in and found you and Garrett and Ed Renke negotiating for the sale of Indian Springs. Garrett thinks Renke took it with him; but I know the man never had that kind of cash or there would have been some of it left when I ran into him, only a couple of weeks later—he'd been running too fast to have got rid of it. And that leaves one candidate.

"So hand over the money—or I'll kill you and find it for myself!"

Downing looked at him, and at the steady gun—the gun that had dropped Tony Balter. It was easy to read his thoughts, in that moment. It was easy to see the fear seep into his cynical brain. He croaked, hoarsely, "It's in the desk, damn you. The upper right-hand drawer—a cigar box—"

Circling carefully, Malloy reached the desk and got the designated drawer open without relaxing his watch on the lawyer.

The box was there, and lifting the lid he found it crammed with large-figured bills. Nodding his satisfaction, he tucked it under one arm.

"I've been on to you quite a spell, mister," he said. "But as long as you thought of me as a thick-headed, tinhorn gambler who could be used to your own purposes, I knew there was no chance of scaring this out of you. It took something flashy—like that performance with Tony Balter just now, out in the dust."

He added, "You meant to let Caslon and the Garretts and me destroy one another, I suppose; then, you'd be around to pick up the pieces. Only, it didn't work out. . . ." He gestured toward the door, with his gunbarrel. "Well, start walking! We're wanted across the street."

Frank Downing began to babble, almost incoherent. "Don't run me in to the law! For the love of God, fellow— can't we make a deal?"

The other's lips twisted in contempt. "I won't waste my time, Frank. When you've finished this job you're free to go to hell, for all I care. Only—I want you gone from Hermit Flats by twelve hours from now. And remember, when *I* set a deadline, I enforce it!"

"I'll go!" cried Downing. "Thanks, Malloy. You're a white man. And you don't have to worry—I'll go!"

"Damn right you will!" And Malloy threw open the door.

His prisoner went hurrying down the steps ahead of him, toward where a crowd had already started to gather in the dust around a certain sprawled and lifeless figure. But for his own part, Mark Malloy had thought then only for Jean Garrett's anxious face and frightened eyes, waiting for him at the bottom of the stairs. . . .

The doctor looked up from a medical journal he had been plodding through; at sight of his visitor he vented a grunt of surprise, and tossed the paper aside, obviously relieved to be quit of it. "I read the damn things," he muttered, indicating the journal with a jerk of his grizzled head, "but all these new-fangled theories they get from the Eastern fellers are plain Greek to an old workhouse like me.

"Well—step in!" Doc Reading added, canting a quizzical look at the man in the doorway. "I hear you been cutting a swath over in that Hermit Flats country. I never expected I'd be seeing you around these parts, any more—thought Saunderstown would shape up a little tame, after the hell-raising you've been up to!"

Mark Malloy shrugged and, pushing away from the door-jamb where he had been leaning, he walked into the room, pulled a chair around and slacked into it. He was dressed once more in the tailored town clothes, and the thin cheroots lined his waistcoat pocket.

He took out a couple of these and passed one across the desk, wincing a little as he did so. "Sore shoulder," he explained. "Had a bullet dug out of it."

Reading was studying him with a piercing glance, as he twisted the cheroot in blunt fingers. "On the go again, ain't you? Funny. I'd heard you had took over some property there on the Flats, and was settling down to be a big-shot rancher!"

"You surely can't mean me," Malloy answered mildly. "Why, Doc, what would I do with a ranch? I went and deeded it over to some people that had more use for it than I ever would. Family named Garrett."

"Get a good bargain?"

The other shrugged again.

"Not a cent. They wanted to pay me, but the old man has a spine operation facing him and I figured he needed his money worse than I did."

"And now, I take it you're heading back to the poker tables."

"Why, a man belongs to what he knows," said Malloy, without conviction. "Which reminds me, Doc, I came here to tell you it's time you should change professions. You're a fraud!"

Reading's stare narrowed on him. "This a joke or something?"

"Not with me, it's no joke! Remember what you said about my eyes bothering me? How I should give them a rest —get some fresh air and exercise, for a week or two, and that that would fix them up?"

"Uh-huh, I remember. So what happened?"

"So they're just as bad as ever! The very first time I sat down to look at a few cards, they went out on me again! How about it, Doc?" he added. "You got any more of your smart ideas?"

The other frowned at him through a long, thoughtful moment, while the street sounds of Saunderstown came lazily from an open window beside the desk. Finally, Reading said, "Malloy, where do you do your eating, mainly? Greasy joints, I suppose, and these small-town hotels?"

"What's that have to do with it?"

"Quite a lot, maybe. This journal I was just reading . . ." He indicated it with a flip of his hand. "Them medicos back East come up with a lot of new-fangled notions, but it don't mean they might not be right, once in a way. And they're saying now the wrong kind of diet can be the real cause of a lot of symptomatic troubles, such as yours.

"So, as nothing else seems to work, could be that's the medicine you need—a steady dosage of real, honest-to-God home cooking, taken three times daily! I'd say it's worth a try."

"Home cooking—?"

Malloy's head had lifted suddenly, an odd expression moving across his face that still held its marks of battle. Reading observed him closely.

"That give you some ideas, maybe?"

"Yeah," the other answered, slowly. "Maybe it does, at that, Doc."

And with his characteristic gambler's fatalism he added, silently, *Why not? What can I lose by asking her?*

True, she'd been furious when he kissed her; she'd said, "It doesn't matter to me if Tony Balter kills you!" But that next morning she'd been on hand to see the shoot-out, and she'd called to him in alarm and fear. Funny, that he hadn't thought of that before. . . .

Mark Malloy drew a deep breath. He knew, somehow, that this would be his last gamble—and that, if he should win it, he stood to win the big prize of all his random restless years.

He came to his feet abruptly. "Thanks, Doc," he said. "Maybe I'll take that advice. Maybe I'll even settle down to ranching—who knows? Stranger things have happened. . . . Wish me luck, will you?"

"Luck?" The doctor shook his head. "That's just a fool gambler's superstition. A man has no luck but what he makes himself!"

Malloy considered this. "Maybe so," he answered. "But maybe not, either." He smiled a little. "Right now, for some reason—I'm feeling awfully lucky!"

He left the office with a quick, impatient stride; for he felt already the pull of the long and dusty miles back to Hermit Flats. Something said he would not be leaving there, ever again.

THE END